# STUCK AT CHRISTMAS

GEORGIA COFFMAN

Stuck at Christmas © 2021 GEORGIA COFFMAN

Dogwood Cove © Julia Jarrett

STUCK AT CHRISTMAS

Editing by Amanda Cuff, Word of Advice Editing
Cover Design by Mae Harden

*For my best friend, Jody. You're one of the strongest women I know, and I love your genuine heart and soul.*

## ONE

GRAHAM

"Either you haven't had enough to drink or you really hate charities," a soothing voice sounds next to me as a flash of wavy brown hair crosses my periphery.

I drag my gaze over the tables covered in white linens. In the middle of each one are centerpieces more decadent than I'd see at a wedding. They match the color scheme of the numerous Christmas trees, which are draped with extravagant holiday garlands that are almost blinding.

But that's how my best friend does this sort of thing. Nothing is too much to celebrate a noble organization, and the charity of honor tonight is definitely that.

Contrary to the woman's second guess, it's part of the reason I'm at this fundraiser right now. My family and I have a close connection with Darby's Dreamers, an organization that helps families adopt children with Down Syndrome. A family friend adopted their two boys with the organization's assistance, and I'm here for support.

As if in slow motion—thanks to the few flutes of champagne I've had—I keep turning until I'm looking at the woman to my right. She's in a deep mauve velvet dress, leaning over the bar and sliding her new drink toward herself as she studies me.

She's the one who came in late. We'd already begun the third course by the time she took her seat at the table next to mine, but her tardiness wasn't what caught my attention like it did many of the other guests.

I noticed her because it was hard not to.

Her dress hugs her body like she's doing it a favor by wearing it, and up close, she's even more stunning.

I tilt my head toward her and plaster a smile on my face. "Excuse me?"

She points a slender finger at me from around the stem of her martini glass. "You look like you've just come out of a Brazilian wax. Like you're in pain."

I raise my eyebrows, my lips twitching. My fingers tremble to pull the suffocating bow tie from around my neck, but her curious once-over stops me.

She holds the toothpick of olives to the side as she sips her drink, then licks her lips, sparkles dancing in her dark brown eyes like fireflies in the evening. "Who made you come out here tonight?"

I turn my attention back to the dance floor as the song comes to an end, and Carter and Tessa pull apart, smiling at each other like loons on their honeymoon. I nod toward them and glance at the woman next to me. "My best friend and little sister. I'm here for the charity, but also for them. Trying to be the bigger man or whatever and be okay with their..." I grind my teeth, biting out the last word. "*Relationship*."

"Glad to see it's going well for you." She smiles, and my witty response gets caught in my throat.

Her beauty is indisputable. She's elegant, and even when she was running late, she was graceful, seemingly uncaring that people were staring. She sat with her head held high as though we had just started eating too early.

Her long, silky chestnut hair cascades around her shoulders in loose waves that appear effortless, but having a sister, I know it probably took a while to achieve that look.

On top of it all, her smile is beyond gorgeous. It lights up her entire face brighter than the chandeliers across the ceiling.

"Are you going to be grumpy all night? If so, I can find someone else to chat up." She lifts one eyebrow in challenge and sips her drink, her gaze never leaving mine.

I crack a crooked grin. "Grumpy?"

Her cheeky smile falters. "Right. That's not exactly how grown-ups talk, huh?"

"What?" I chuckle, furrowing my brows.

"Graham, there you are." Tessa appears to my left, taking me by surprise. "Dance with us."

"Why?" I ask warily as I set my drink on the bar, already moving toward her. She's my sister. No matter how pissed I am that she's now dating my best friend, I can never say no to her or stay mad at her forever.

I hate to say it, but I can't be mad at Carter for the next fifty years, either, like I previously wanted to. He's groveled for weeks.

*Weeks.*

I thought he would've thrown in the towel after a couple days, but he's been texting, calling, and wanting to meet me for coffee or dinner for weeks.

I did finally accept an in-person meeting with him—I could only use my busy schedule at the clinic as an excuse for so long. The truth is, my job as a physician does keep me busy, but it's not like I can't get away for coffee, at the very least.

"Carter's schmoozing guests—aka moneybags—and I wanted to dance with you, anyway. It's not a crime to want to spend time with my brother." She shrugs, pulling me onto the dance floor.

I glance over my shoulder to excuse myself from the intriguing woman, but she's no longer there. Neither is her drink.

*Damn.* I didn't even get her name.

I hold Tessa's hand and sway to the music with her. Over her head, I search the crowded room for a sinful velvet dress and soft curls I'd love to tangle my hands in, but I come up empty. When did so many people get here? It's like searching the flecks of snow on the ground outside.

"Carter did a good job filling the room up," Tessa says, then spins under my arm.

When she's facing me again, I say, "That's exactly what I was thinking. Did I say it out loud?"

"No." She giggles, and her eyes shine. "You know me well, but guess what, brother? I know you too. Although I've never seen you drink as much as you have tonight." Her amused expression falters as she eyes me, and it's obvious she's silently urging me to explain myself.

I let go of her waist to dig the heel of my palm over one eye, then resume dancing, my gaze still traveling over the room for the mystery woman.

"Graham?" Tessa squeezes my hand, drawing my attention back to her. "You sure you're okay with this? With Carter and me?"

I shake my head, which makes me dizzy. I've had several drinks—mostly the ones I downed when I first walked in here—and they must all be hitting me at once. I thought I had eaten enough to settle my buzz, but no such luck. I smile down at Tessa and squeeze her hand back. "I'll be fine with you and my best friend." I roll my eyes at that last part. "But I need some water. And air. I had more to drink than I thought."

She nods, stepping away as her hands slide back to her sides. "I'll get you some water."

"Not necessary." I glance over her shoulder at Carter. "Your *boyfriend* is cutting in."

"One of these days, you're going to have to say it without cringing." Carter stares pointedly at me, a sharp gleam in his eyes.

"We'll see," I challenge, narrowing my gaze.

I mess with him some more, drudging up dirt I have on him. Given that I've known the guy since college—over fifteen years—I know *a lot*.

After a good laugh down memory lane, I leave them to slow dance and make out like no one's watching.

I'm dealing with their new relationship in my own way, but I can't deny how happy they both look tonight. It's more obvious than a common cold.

Not that I think their relationship is the equivalent of a sniffling, boogered mess, but like I said—I'm dealing.

Doesn't mean I can't give my best friend hell in the process.

I fidget with my bow tie and jacket as I make my way outside—I'm more suited for an open white coat than a restrictive tux. Before I reach the doors, a server offers me champagne, but I shake my head and decline.

Water is in my best interest right now. I'm not drunk, but I'm definitely too buzzed to drive myself home. Thankfully, Carter sent a car, which I have to admit was a thoughtful gesture.

People, especially the media around this area, like to speculate that he's an irresponsible billionaire, but I've known him for far too long and can't agree. He might be an ass on occasion, but he's always been more than his bank account, which also helps alleviate the headache he's caused by dating my sister.

In the hall outside the event room, I shuffle to a station set up with water. I fill a cup to the brim and down it, letting the cool and refreshing liquid stream down my throat like a waterfall.

I grab another and walk along the paisley carpet toward the double doors, which I hope will lead me to fresh air.

Once I push them open, I find more than that.

*The mystery woman.*

She stands with her back to me, her hair lightly swaying in the chilling wind. She leans over the rail, and the city stretches beyond her, the lights of New York twinkling all around like stars across the sky. Which is nice since we can't see the actual stars above, not with all the light pollution from the city.

I study her silhouette, and as I inch closer, I note how tense she Is. She seems lost in thought and uncaring that she's shivering. It's December, after all, and although it's taking a break for now, snow has been falling all day.

As I approach, I shrug my jacket off. "You're either upset or you really hate charities," I say, my voice unintentionally raspy.

When she looks up at me, her expression softens. Her frown transforms into a smile as she accepts my jacket and wraps it around her shoulders. "It's the first one, but I'd rather not talk about it." She turns to face the city again.

I nod, rocking on my heels and steeling myself against the rush of wind that swoops between us.

"Your friend in there—Carter? You seemed to have

patched things up with him." She raises her arm to lean her elbow on the rail and rests her chin in her palm.

I dip my head, stiffening again as another cold gust whips through my short hair. "We'll be fine, but I'm not done giving him a hard time."

She raises her eyebrows.

Sighing, I lean my elbows on the rail next to her and clasp my fingers together. My words escape in a quick rush like I'm afraid they won't come out otherwise. "He was always the arrogant one of our group. In college, he was the one ladies flocked to even before they knew he was a billionaire. And now my sister is one of them. She's like a groupie."

The woman covers her mouth with her dainty left hand as she giggles, and although the adorable sound briefly catches my attention—it's a youthful laugh that echoes pleasantly over the city noise—I zero in on her bare ring finger.

"It's not funny," I manage and clear my throat.

"It is a little," she says as she holds her thumb and forefinger an inch apart. Dropping her arm, she angles her body to face me. "If it's any help, I think Carter's a good guy. He gets a bad rap from the media, but he's done so much to help various charities. He doesn't just make donations, either. Like tonight—one of his goals is to raise awareness. He invited journalists and reporters to cover the event, and he sent brochures and such to the magazines that couldn't send reps."

"Shit, maybe you should date him," I grumble as my frown sets in place like a bad tattoo.

She throws her head back and laughs as if it's a ridiculous suggestion, which makes me relax. "No, no, no." She waves her hand in front of her face. "Just no."

I spin and lean my back against the rail, eyeing the red

tint on her nose like that of a certain reindeer. "What's your name?"

She turns her gaze up to meet mine, her expression coy as she seemingly fights a smile. "Now, why would you want to know such a thing?"

"So I can include it in my phone when you give me your number." I wink, grinning like I've already gotten her information typed and saved into my contacts.

"And here I thought Carter was the arrogant one." She tsks. The twinkle in her eyes grows brighter and more mischievous as she says, "What if we don't exchange names?"

Disappointment settles in the pit of my stomach, but it's quickly replaced by intrigue. What is she saying?

"I'm sorry?" I lean in, and my fingertips are mere inches from her, itching to wrap themselves around her hip and pull her closer.

She meets me halfway, her body melting against mine as she takes on a hooded and confident expression that wasn't there before. "What if we have a little *fun*, instead? No names or obligations attached?" she suggests, her voice low and seductive.

I blink, then drop my attention to her fingers that wrap around my loosened bow tie and pull it the rest of the way undone.

The bustling city below us seems to freeze, along with the dew on cars and the once-swaying limbs of the few trees lining the sidewalks.

*I* freeze.

For a moment, it's like my blood stills in my veins.

But as she grips the ends of my bow tie and tugs me down toward her face, my body comes alive again.

Blood rushes south.

Nerve endings fire.

Anticipation jolts me into action.

She lifts onto her tiptoes, her lips parted and ready for me, and I give in to this strong temptation.

I capture her mouth with mine, grazing my lips across hers and reveling in the rush of kissing a stranger. My kiss is easy at first, slow and deliberate as I savor her.

She tastes of mint, like she's just eaten a candy cane, and the faintest hint of vodka is there too. I lap it all up as I sweep my tongue across her soft bottom lip.

This night has taken a turn for the better, indeed.

I smooth her hair back with both hands until I'm cradling her head and angling it so that I can dive my tongue deeper into her welcoming mouth.

A soft whimper escapes her as she sighs with content and wraps her arms around my waist.

I take one step toward her, closing the tiny gap between us and pulling her flush against me as I explore her mouth like I'll find answers to solve the mystery of this woman.

She's fucking sexy and sweet.

Responsive and dizzying.

Her hand flies to my neck, gripping the back of it like it's her tether to this building so she doesn't fall over the side of it, and our kiss turns frantic.

I wrap my arms around her waist, the tent between my legs now rock-hard and so damn obvious.

She pulls back with a gasp, her red lipstick smudged across the top, hiding the dip of her swollen bowed lips. "I have an idea," she rasps, her eyelids heavy with desire.

I nod so fast it makes me lightheaded.

She grabs my hand and whirls around, but I stop us as an important thought pierces through to the forefront of my foggy brain. "Wait—how much have you had to drink?"

"One and a half martinis. I get more drunk off whiskey-glazed pork. You?"

"Drunk enough not to risk driving myself home, but sober enough to perform CPR if needed."

Biting her lip, she grabs my hand again and marches toward the event hall like she's on a mission. And I fucking follow her like it's my last day on Earth.

When we enter the crowded space, Michael Bublé's cover of "White Christmas" is muffled by my thundering heart in my ears, and as we slip past the guests, down the hall toward an empty closet, I'm sure I've died.

Once we rush inside, she clicks the door shut and leans her back against it, facing me.

Inviting me to continue what we started outside.

The smell and dim light above us allow me to note we're in a custodial closet. If I checked, I'm certain I'd find mops, bleach, and other cleaning supplies.

But I don't stop.

I hardly think about anything at all, other than the subtle hardening of this captivating woman's nipples, which is more and more visible the longer we stare at each other. Running my tongue along my lips to wet them, I step toward her and capture her mouth with mine again, relishing the silence.

I'm not normally one for casual hookups—in a dusty closet, no less—but she's an exception.

Tonight, I indulge in a fantasy with this person I've never met. One whose name I don't even know. But she's a woman I already know I'll never forget.

## TWO

## ISABEL

W hat am I doing?

Am I really making out with a random man in a dark closet?

He squeezes my hands by my sides, then brings his up to tangle them in my hair as if he's waited all night to do just that. The strong tingling sensations it causes makes me sag against the door, bringing him with me.

It's like he's dedicated himself to curing a deep ache in my core I didn't even know existed until I laid eyes on him.

He's the perfect mix of handsome and charming, like a rich and delicious chocolate peppermint martini.

When I decided to make an appearance at this event— my first real social outing since Heath—I didn't expect to have any fun, let alone end up in a closet with a man whose name I insisted I didn't need.

My God, I'm the one who instigated this.

I blame his crooked grin. He'd been brooding and scowling until I spoke my first words to him, and when he finally cracked a smile, I melted.

It transformed him, softening his sharp jaw, and it

seemed like it was a smile he didn't often flash, which made me feel special. Like I'd accomplished some magical feat.

Or maybe it's just that I've been watching too many soap operas or listening to Blair tell too many stories of her newly single life. Turns out, men like a woman who gets waxed regularly and has a large bank account—or seven, like Blair.

I didn't need to pull the money card with this guy. First of all, he's friends with Carter Fields, billionaire extraordinaire, and his tux is Gucci. He doesn't seem like the kind of guy to be impressed by the green paper.

The truth, though, is that I didn't want to play the wealthy divorcée bit. Just this once, I want to be someone other than the bitter single mother who's always running late and spends most of her time picking up her six-year-old's *Frozen* and *Miraculous* dolls after having stepped on them repeatedly.

Still, no matter how justified I am in wanting to hook up with a sexy stranger, this is so unlike me, and I shouldn't—

He nips at my bottom lip, working it between his teeth like a wild animal. He's hungry for me. His kisses are firm and purposeful, and all rational thoughts are pushed aside like they're whisked away in a blizzard.

His warm body pressed against mine feels too good. His kisses are firm and purposeful. His grip possessive. When was the last time I felt like this? So *wanted* by a man?

I grip his neck with both hands and kiss him back with fervor, savoring the taste of him. It's like he soaked his tongue in champagne, and I lap it up with my own as I stand on my tiptoes.

I keep rising until his hard length is pressed between my legs.

*Bingo.*

"Oh, yes," I breathe, but our mouths are so smashed together, the syllables are lost.

He grunts, sliding his hand over my hip, to my ass, and down to wrap it behind my knee. Hiking my leg up, he pushes into me, and my eyes roll into the back of my head.

That's it—I've officially left this planet.

I've left it on this guy's sexy biceps like he's a magic carpet.

This has to be the Christmas miracle I've been wishing for.

After the worst damn year of my life, this guy is my reward, and I plan on taking full advantage. Besides, he's obviously more than willing, if his hardness is any indication.

And holy hell on a gingerbread cookie, he's *hard*.

I suck in a sharp breath as his fingers glide over the bare skin of my exposed arms and shoulders, lighting me on fire. "I want you," I whisper as he licks his way up the column of my neck.

"I was just going to say the same." He moves his mouth back to mine, planting a hard kiss there as he slides his hand underneath my dress.

He explores his way up to the lace of my panties, leaving a trail of prickly goose bumps along my inner thigh.

I'm trembling with anticipation.

Out of breath.

Drowning in this game of seduction with a charming man I don't know.

The allure of it all turns me on in ways I've never experienced, and when this guy dips his finger inside me, I'm a goner.

I buck my hips into his as he curls his finger, and my

pulsing heat clenches around him. Beside us, a broom or mop falls over, clamoring to the floor, but it doesn't faze us.

I cling to his lean frame as he continues working me, his lips staying on mine. He swallows gasp after gasp as I relish in this new feeling of being worshipped.

Because that's what he's doing.

He's kissing and touching me like I'm the most valuable thing to him in the world.

"Right there." I jolt back, and my head hits the door with delicious pain as he finds that special spot at the right angle with the perfect amount of pressure.

He doesn't know me, and yet, he's touching me like he knows every little secret of mine.

I tug on the ends of his sandy blond hair as he brings me to the brink, his expert finger working me into a stupor, where all I see are stars brighter than Christmas tree toppers. Right when I think I can't take it anymore, he pulls back, and my hands fly to his waist. Through my lusty fog, I fumble until I finally yank his cummerbund up, my fingers trembling with need as he kisses my neck, his labored breaths hot against my skin.

I hum as urgency racks my body, and I undo the button of his trousers like I'm searching for gold. "Please tell me you have a condom," I plead hoarsely, my chest heaving.

I feel his smile form against my collarbone, and he reaches inside his jacket pocket for a black leather wallet. "I didn't expect this to happen, but luckily, I'm always prepared, given what I do for—"

I cut him off with a kiss, unable to stop the desire from pooling in my core and fueling my actions. "Hurry," I pant.

His growl echoes throughout my entire body as he rushes to sheath himself. Once he's done, his pants bunched around his corded thighs, he hikes my dress up and removes my panties with earnest vigor.

My legs tremble as he grabs each of them from the outside and hoists me up to wrap myself around him. With my back against the door, he plunges into me, his length sliding effortlessly into my wet heat.

This is a level of turned on I've never been before.

Not even when Heath and I first started dating in college —when we were extra hormonal and crazy about each other—did I feel this frenzied.

This man swivels his hips in perfect rhythm, angling himself deep inside me and surprising me with how well my body responds to him.

My core clenches around him, welcoming him, and I get lost in the sensation.

He pulls and pushes.

Slides and tugs.

Grabs and teases.

He's doing so much at once, I'm delirious and mumbling incoherently into his ear, my cheek pressed to his smooth jawline.

"Fuck, you feel..." he strains and growls in my ear when I thread my fingers through his hair, scraping my acrylic nails across his head. "Good," he finishes on a pant.

All I can manage is a moan as he continues moving inside me, the tension in my lower stomach building with each thrust.

My heels dig into his back, pulling at his dress shirt.

All I want is release. Yet, I want to make this elation last forever.

"Ah!" I dip my head, my jaw dropping, and I do something I've never done before—I bite down through the crisp material covering his shoulder. He probably can't even feel it, so I bite harder, which muffles my moans.

After another roll of his hips, I squeeze my legs and release the tension, my entire body screaming and rejoicing as waves of pleasure course through me.

"God, yes." He groans and his body goes slack, sagging against mine as he pumps his release while still inside me.

He pulls back and moves the hair out of my face with the gentlest touch—the complete opposite of his animalistic movements from seconds ago.

I close my eyes and feel his warm lips meet mine in a kiss so beautiful it reaches inside my chest and tugs. In some ways, it's more world-shattering than what we just did.

I gulp when he moves farther back and pulls out. Once he helps set me back on my feet, I finally open my eyes as reality slowly sets in.

The people outside this closet and down the hall. The music. The party. The fundraiser and every last gossip of what used to be my inner circle until Heath and I split.

I bring my hand up to my heated cheek and follow the guy's movements as he disposes of the condom into a trash bag. As he slides his pants back up and into place, he squints to study me, but I don't meet his gaze head-on. Instead, I grab my panties from the floor and stuff them into my bra, my heart rate spiking. He opens his mouth to speak, but I cut him off, my words rushed. "I need to go."

"Wait, I don't even—"

I swing the door open and race down the hall, picking up the side of my dress to avoid tripping over it. That's just what I need—falling on my face as I try to get away from the best sex I've ever had.

It was a spontaneous suggestion.

A fun escape from reality.

It wasn't supposed to be as damn magical as it was.

At the check-in counter, I frantically ask for my coat, then hurry down the hall and burst through the doors of the venue. I scurry down the steps, pulling my phone from my coat pocket, and once I reach the safety of the sidewalk, I call Neal to bring the car around.

"Can I help you, miss?" a valet asks as he approaches.

"I have it under control." I nod and force a smile, repeating those words to myself for many other reasons.

Within seconds, Neal curves the black town car around the circle drive and up to where I stand. I barely hear a voice from the top of the stairs calling out for me to wait, and I know it's *his* voice.

His plea.

But I don't stop.

Neal turns to me from the driver's seat. "I think he's speaking to you, Miss Michaels."

I give him a sad smile. "Please take me home."

## THREE

## GRAHAM

I step over the threshold and feel like I'm entering a Christmas wonderland instead of my parents' house.

Cotton pretending to be snow is stretched and fluffed across the entryway table, and on top sits a small village, the pieces of which have been collected over the last few years. The railing of the staircase is wrapped in garland and twinkling lights, and red felt mats are stuck across the front of each step.

I'm about to turn the corner and brace myself for the rest of the Christmas décor—my parents' retirement means they have time and energy to churn out more DIY projects from Pinterest decorating blogs—but I don't make it past the doorframe when "Frosty the Snowman" comes to life through their speaker. In my head, though, it comes to a screeching halt like a broken record.

They played this song the night of the fundraiser.

Tessa skirts across my view, short hair flying backward, but she doesn't see me. Carter, on the other hand, comes toward me with a shit-eating grin. Fuck, I want to wipe it off his face like I do snow from my windshield each morning.

"Hey, hot doc." He slaps my back, and I steel myself for more inquiry of my hookup with the mystery woman a few nights ago. "I almost didn't recognize you with that glow in your cheeks. Get any more action—"

"Keep your voice down," I hiss, glancing into the living room to make sure my parents and sister haven't noticed us yet.

The other night, the bastard knew exactly what I'd been up to before I confessed because of the "dazed look in my eyes"—whatever the hell that meant.

Once Carter was done razzing on me like the fraternity brothers we used to be, he said he was happy I found someone. The truth is, the mystery woman was the first person I'd been with in several months.

I work a lot, which doesn't allow for much time to go out and meet people, especially when my parents insist on getting together a few times a month now. I only have so much social energy in me.

*Christ, I sound like a fucking grandpa.*

Carter squeezes my shoulder in his wolfish palm, then lets go, but his eyes remain glued on me. "Are you sure you don't want me to tell you who she is?"

Instantly, I tense, and at the same moment, the music switches songs, silencing us as I gather my wits. "I'm sure," I say, brushing past him.

"Graham!" My mother sets a pitcher of eggnog on the table and rounds the corner toward me, arms open.

I squeeze her in a tight embrace. "Hey, Mom."

"You're late." She pulls back, one eyebrow quirked.

I chuckle. "And you guys never let me forget it."

She smacks my shoulder. "I'm talking about *tonight*."

"I'm talking about every night. And day. And morning.

Tell me, is there a reason you had to have French toast at seven in the morning on a Wednesday?"

"It was *one* time, and we learned our lesson: no more family breakfasts. We're sticking to dinner during the week or lunch on the weekends for you." Mom winks, then saunters back toward the kitchen, leaving me with Carter again.

I grunt before I even turn around, feeling his knowing smirk creep over me like ants crawling on my skin. "What?" I ask, placing both hands on my hips.

"Relax. You aren't about to give a jury your defense."

"I'm not a lawyer."

He rolls his eyes and holds his hands up. "It was just an expression."

"It wasn't relevant." I blink, standing my ground—anything to avert his claws from sinking into the subject of a certain intriguing woman.

Carter rubs a hand down his face. "You're impossible."

I ease my stance, hating how squirmy I am over *her*. "And you're—"

"Why won't you let me give you her name and number? You know you want to call her."

"Of course, I do," I blurt. Exasperated, I exhale, but it doesn't make me feel better. Tension still grabs hold of my shoulders and chest. "But—"

"Graham, there you are!" Tessa comes out of the kitchen with a bowl of gourmet popcorn between her hands, which she sets on the sparkling red tablecloth next to the eggnog station.

My mom stepped it up this year. Instead of just a pitcher of the holiday drink, she's set the table up with matching glasses that look more like small bowls, a mason jar of cinnamon sticks, a tiny cannister of nutmeg, and a bottle of brandy.

My attention settles on the brandy—I could use a drink.

Itching to get away from the conversation with Carter, I meet my sister halfway and wrap my arms around her.

"You're late," she mumbles into my shoulder.

I throw my head back and laugh. "You sound more like Mom every day."

"I'll take that as a compliment." She steps toward Carter and stands on her tiptoes to kiss his cheek.

Instinctively, I shield my eyes with one hand. "Yeah, still not used to that."

Tessa giggles as she shrugs, and no matter how weird this still is for me, I've never seen my sister happier.

Everything from her wavy blonde hair to her rosy cheeks and the animated use of her hands as she talks makes her glow brighter than all of Mom's shiny tree ornaments put together.

I rub the middle of my sternum, a sinking feeling settling there like hail in a thunderstorm—fast and terrifying.

"Did you see the guy who tried to break the lights on the tree at Rockefeller Center last week?" Tessa asks us, but it sounds muffled as my mind drifts.

"Didn't he cast a line with a fishing pole to try and tear them down?" Carter shakes his head.

"He did!" Tessa covers her mouth as she lets out a high-pitched giggle.

Carter snickers. "A real Christmas bandit."

"Or the ghost of Christmas thieves." Tessa leans into him, and they laugh like they're so proud of themselves for this impromptu comedy sketch.

"Someone could've gotten hurt, you know," I quip. "That fishing hook could've taken someone's eye out."

They both turn to me. "There was no hook on it," they say in unison, freaking me out further.

And it makes them laugh harder.

Normally, I'd laugh too, but a sudden weight now sinks in the pit of my stomach as I recall the woman from the fundraiser.

She was witty and confident.

Her curves were soft and sexy.

She was insatiable, and ever since I was between her thighs, I haven't been able to stop thinking about her.

And it's more than the thrill of acting out of character.

I step backward and make my way to the kitchen where my mother scurries between counters. Staying out of her way, I sidle along one side toward the platters, bowls, and dishes for our dinner. "Didn't you say I was late?" I ask sarcastically.

She wipes her hands on her apron that's covered in snowmen and glances up, her lips slightly twitching. "You were. And we knew it would happen, so we took our time cooking."

"Touché." I scratch my chin and shrug. "I am really sorry. I ran long with a patient."

She waves me off. "Trust me, I know how it is. Your father was the same."

I nod. "Need any help?"

"I'd love if you could take some of these dishes to the table. It's all ready."

"Where's Dad?" I ask over my shoulder as I grab the large platter of turkey, which is decorated with green garnish and red cherry tomatoes like berries of holly.

She points toward the ceiling. "Upstairs. He's icing his hip."

"From falling last week?" I stop in my tracks, the turkey growing heavy in my hands.

"What's going on?" Tessa appears in the doorway, her eyebrows furrowed.

"Dad still isn't feeling well." I set the platter back down, my jaw clenched. "I should go check on him."

"He's fine." My mother waves her hands. "He's icing it only as a precaution. He wants to make sure he's well enough for the holidays." She unties her apron and adjusts her silk blouse, smiling warmly, which puts me at ease—but only a fraction. "I'll go get him, and you'll see for yourself that he is just fine."

"I would like to see for myself," I retort, keeping my tone light, even though I'm concerned.

I checked him out at the clinic myself, and he was okay in the sense that nothing's broken and just bruised from where he fell.

But it doesn't mean his injury hasn't turned into something more serious.

I exhale, roughly running my hands over my face.

"Hey." Tessa rubs her palms up and down my arms. "Have you been sleeping okay? You look tired."

"As opposed to what I normally look like—bubbly and relaxed like a fresh mimosa?" I let out a soft laugh.

She tilts her head and twists her lips. "I'm serious."

"Thank you, sis, but you don't need to worry about me. You've got your hands full with that one, anyway." I nod toward the direction where Carter just entered, and I smirk when he flips me off behind her back. "Besides, it's the holiday season. Cheer and all that shit. What's not to be okay about?"

Tessa nods, but the crease between her brows remains. I

know her well enough to see she's not convinced, but this isn't her problem.

I offer her a small smile as I grab the turkey again and take it to the dining room since the kitchen's starting to feel cramped. There's shuffling behind me, so I know they're following.

Carter has a bowl of roasted potatoes in one hand and a cheesy casserole in the other, and Tessa's on his heel as he says to me, "You could be even more okay if you'd let me give you her—"

"Watch it," I growl as my sister flings her gaze at me.

Carter's smirk spreads slowly and dangerously, and I know I'm not going to like what happens next. It's the look he gave me in college when he came up with the brilliant plan to break into our own house once we realized we both somehow lost our keys. When the cops arrived—thanks to the high-and-mighty neighborhood watch—Carter charmed our way out of an arrest, but I still never let him forget that he almost cost me a smudge on my record.

He nods toward the front door. "Let's chat."

"We're about to eat." I wave over the food.

Tessa's gaze bounces between us as Carter says, "This won't take long."

I mutter under my breath as I follow him out to the front stoop. Once the door is shut behind us, I stuff my hands into my pockets and bounce in place as snow leisurely falls, a soft white dust settling on my shoulders.

"Tell me what's going on," Carter presses.

"Why are you insisting on this?" I peer at him. "As I've said many times, you and I are square about my sister. You don't have to keep trying so hard."

He waves me off, laughing. "I know we're good. Besides, people can't stay mad at me for too long, anyway." He flashes me the grin that's landed him on the covers of magazines, and I just shake my head. What else can I do? "This is about you. It's been, what, six months since you last went on a date, let alone did anything... *else*." He winks, the ever-present twinkle in his eyes irritating me almost as much as this conversation.

I grumble and avert my gaze to the neighboring houses, but their Christmas wreaths and lights wrapped around their stoop railings become a blur.

"Besides, you've always been there for me, and I want to do the same for you. I don't see what the problem is if I just give you her name. I could—"

"Please, for the love of God, do you ever shut up?" I throw my head back, then turn to him, my shoulders deflating. "Fine. You win. Here's the truth."

He rubs his hands together, shifting on his feet, his grin wide and victorious.

I laugh under my breath, but then sober as I say, "She ran off."

"What?" He freezes with his hands in a prayer-like manner in front of his chest.

"After we hooked up, she ran off like she couldn't get away from me fast enough." I glance up at him, then hash out the rest of the sordid tale—the ugly parts I left out when I originally told him of my rendezvous. All I said before was that we didn't exchange names and that it was a one-time thing.

Now, it's all coming out. I tell Carter about how badly I wanted to get her name. How spontaneous and exhilarating that night was because of her. She brought out the daring and fun side of me that I hadn't seen in years, and I wanted more of it.

I *want* more.

By the time I'm done talking, I feel pathetic. When have I ever whined like this over a woman? Not even in junior high did I pine after a girl as badly as I am right now.

"You know what"—I brush past him toward the door and twist the knob—"forget it. I'm being ridiculous. It was just sex. Nothing special, obviously. She didn't feel the same, and that's the end of the story. I'm going inside."

I'm almost to sweet freedom when Carter's voice sounds again. "Oh my God."

"What?" I spin toward him, his tone grating on my nerves. He said it like I'm stupid, and it pisses me off.

"It's the pride thing." He crosses his arms, remaining on the second step down on the stoop. Even though I'm towering over him, I feel small, and it angers me further.

"What pride thing?" I grind out, opening and closing my fists by my sides.

"*Your* pride thing." He hops up to where I stand by the door and claps my shoulder. "I mean, last year, you actually stopped taking the subway because someone once pushed you out of the way to take your seat."

"It was rude." I glare at him, my eye twitching as I fight the urge to point out that, unlike for him, public transit is sometimes a necessity. I'm a doctor with an overflowing patient load and I'm doing well for myself, but taking the subway is the only solution when my car is in the shop or traffic is too much.

And it's hardly ever a pleasant experience.

"I agree." He holds his hands up, the top of his head now damp from the snow melting against it.

Running a hand through my own hair, I say, "We're going to get sick if we stay out here much longer like this, so you better make your point soon."

"You haven't taken the subway in months, even though

it's your fastest option most of the time. Instead of just getting the fuck over it, you're taking a losing stance just because of your pride. So, when—not if, but *when*—you realize I'm right, I'll tell you her name." His breath comes out in soft puffs much like my own, and then, he breaks into a wide grin. "There. Now I'm done."

I clench my jaw as I follow him inside, immediately relieved when the warmth washes over me. Brushing past him, I make my way to the bar and pour myself a full glass of whiskey.

"Hey, you have the Christmas Wrap-Up charity event this week, right?" Tessa asks Carter as I join them by the dinner table.

He nods, then turns to me. "Care to join us? Just think of all this"—Carter waves his hand up and down the front of me—"holiday cheer you'll spread."

"Thanks, asshole." I take a hefty sip of my whiskey with zero finesse. It's more like a country lumberjack, especially when the liquid drips down my chin and I wipe it with my sleeve. "Since when did you become a hands-on kind of billionaire philanthropist, anyway?"

"Since always." He winks at me. "It seems more cameras arrive when I'm present, which bodes well for the causes."

I mutter a curse because he's right, and it's definitely beneficial in bringing awareness to each cause. *The generous bastard.*

"See?" My mother finally appears with my dad next to her. "He's in one healthy, albeit grumpy, piece, and he's fine."

"I'd be better if the assholes next door would stop using our trash bins as their own. I see the tall one stashing cans of beer in ours like he's afraid his woman will notice how much he drinks to put up with her." He winks.

"Is that your way of telling me *we* spend too much time

together?" My mom puts both hands on her hips and narrows her gaze at Dad, a playful gleam in her eyes.

He pulls her into his arms and kisses her cheek. "Never."

"Retirement is still going well, then, I see." I nod, my lips a tight line of aggravation.

*I want what they have.*

I want the playful and loving relationship they boast.

Rubbing my aching chest, I cross the dining room toward the kitchen and lean on the counter. Where the hell is this coming from?

My family and friends have tried setting me up with every single woman they know and meet, but I've always dismissed them because I'm not ready. I'm still fairly new to the medical world, working at the clinic with my father's old partner who refuses to admit he'll need to retire soon as well. There's a lot of pressure associated with being a thirty-five-year-old physician, and I can't risk getting clobbered by it.

It's why I work so hard and insist on the long hours—to earn my place there. To be an asset for the city. To live my calling.

The practice has always been my excuse to stay away from any serious relationship, but this is the first time I've been bothered by what I might be missing.

My family's chatter grows louder and floats into the kitchen as I continue idly scratching my chest over my button down.

I close my eyes, taken back to the buzz of the charity dinner a few nights ago as I held the mystery woman's hand, my finger drawing circles on her smooth palm.

Her purring in my ear as we gave ourselves to each other in that closet.

Her leg wrapped around my waist, and the way she bit my shoulder with raw intensity.

The more I think about her, the more tempted I am to ask Carter who she is, but as the memories continue flooding my mind, I can't help but stop myself.

She left.

She ran away from me when I tried to ask for her name and number.

And it stung more than I care to admit.

Is Carter right? Do I have too much pride?

Being rejected by her fucking stung. I thought it was because I really liked her, but maybe it's a mix of that and the fact that my ego took a bigger hit than a fragile tree in an avalanche.

"Graham?" Tessa pokes her head into the kitchen. "We're about to eat, and you don't want to keep Dad waiting. He's extra feisty tonight. I think his cured hip is making him feel invincible."

Chuckling, I push off the counter and follow her back to the dining room.

But even as we eat, talk easily, and prepare a holiday plan for exchanging presents and visiting the family cabin, the ache in my chest remains. Even though I have friends and family, something's missing.

There's a hole in my life, and I've never wanted to fill it until now.

## FOUR

ISABEL

O ne happy little family.

That's what we look like in the picture in my hand—Sasha, her father, and me with wide smiles in front of our house in the Hamptons. Sasha had just turned two and didn't know what it meant to be there, standing in front of such a house with a spectacular view.

One that was ours.

It's what Heath and I always talked about. When we met in college and quickly became inseparable, he and I fantasized about the big, fancy jobs we'd get in Manhattan and all the things we'd do: travel internationally, buy a splendid vacation home somewhere as coveted as the Hamptons, and have a family.

We did all those things and added an extra: *divorce*.

Now, he's traveling the world and spending weekends at the Hampton home with a different woman every week.

While I resort to a one-night stand at a charity dinner.

The thought of the extraordinary man from that night immediately makes me blush, and I touch my flushed cheek with the back of my hand as I recall the way he gripped my hips. It was like he refused to let me go.

When was the last time a man made me feel so important? So sexy and one of a kind? Before that night, I'm not sure I ever felt that way.

Not even Heath had that powerful of an effect on me.

In college, he and I couldn't keep our hands off each other, but it was the clumsy kind of attraction that's common at a young age. It's nothing like the undeniable desire and expert touch I experienced from the curious man with piercing blue eyes, and we didn't even know each other's names.

I scoot the picture frame back in its place on Sasha's dresser as my mother comes in, holding a piece of paper out to me. "Sweetheart, what's this flyer about Christmas Wrap-Up? I saw it on the fridge."

I smile, knowing the event well. "It's a volunteer opportunity to wrap toys for children. I participated last year, and it was extremely rewarding." I recall how Carter's presence at the event had brought even more publicity to the cause, and we'd doubled the number of donated gifts compared to the previous year. "I'm going to take Sasha once she's done with rehearsal. I thought we could make it a family tradition, starting this year."

"Sounds marvelous." My mother claps. "I'll get my coat."

I giggle. "Sasha won't be done for another hour. There's no rush."

"All right, then." She waves for me to follow her out into the hall. "Let's have some wine. We'll take a cab to get Sasha."

"We're not showing up to volunteer with my daughter while drunk." I quirk a brow. My mother's always been cooky, but since my father passed a couple years ago, she's become even more so.

Once we reach the kitchen, she sighs and grabs a bottle of Cabernet from the wine rack above the sink. "Fine. I'll have a glass and you'll drive. Until then, talk to me."

"Sasha's play is next week. Don't be late." I narrow my gaze at her, knowing she's also become very poor with time management lately. She seems to live by her own clock.

"Like you're any better at being punctual," she teases.

"You know how hard it is to get out of the house on time when a child is involved."

She smiles like she does know, indeed, and takes a sip, then licks her lips. "I already have the play in my planner. I mean, *talk* to me. You've been doing a lot of meditation and daydreaming, and it seems like you need to let it out. So, let's have it." She waves for me to answer her, although I'm not sure what she expects.

"I haven't been daydreaming. Just thinking is all." I shrug, moving around her toward the fridge. Tugging the door open, I reach inside for the cheese platter I made up last night, set it on the table, and uncover it for us.

She grabs a chunk of gouda and toys with it as she glares at me, her expression full of doubt. It's the same one she'd give me when she wanted the truth out of me, whether it was to out Dad for stealing a piece of turkey before dinner or if I scraped my leg because I missed curfew and had to climb through the window.

"You know everything, don't you?" I joke, unable to stop myself from smiling.

"Of course." She shrugs with an underlying *duh* in her tone.

"I was thinking is all," I repeat, shaking my head and reaching for a piece of aged cheddar.

She sighs again, obviously exasperated with my non-answer. But what can I say? How can I tell my mother I've been busy daydreaming about a guy I hooked up with at a charity dinner like it was a frat party? It's less than becoming of a lady, to say the least, and my mother would flip.

Although, she's changed a lot since I was a teenager. At this point, she might even cheer for me.

Oh, God—would she ask for details?

Bad idea all around.

"Do you know what Sasha asked me yesterday?" my mother asks, leaning her hip against the edge of the island.

"Did she mention anything about the play? Her costume is a little big around the shoulders."

"She asked me what *mating for life* means."

I choke on my own spit. "What the h—" Through my racing thoughts, I manage to catch myself, stealing a peek at my mother. She doesn't seem to have noticed that I was about to curse, paying more attention to the funnel of red liquid she creates by swirling her glass in small circles. *She has certainly changed.* "Where did she learn that?"

"I'd say it was from you and all your *daydreaming*," she says sarcastically and sips her wine, a twinkle in her eye as she watches me over the rim.

Ignoring her jab, I press, "What did you tell her? A six-year-old does not need to know that."

"I agree," she says too easily. "So I told her to ask you."

"What?" I lean forward like she hit me in the stomach.

"My time in life to give the birds and the bees talk is over." She lifts an eyebrow as I all but pick my jaw up off the floor. "Your turn."

She continues sipping her wine like she didn't just drop a bomb on me. My daughter is only six. I have not prepared myself for the teenage years, and it seems they've started early.

I'm about to snatch the glass from my mother—I need that wine more than she does—when my vibrating phone buzzing on the island between us interrupts. My stomach sinks when I see it's the school calling, and I swipe to answer.

"Mrs. Murray? It's Vice Principal Hamilton," her nasally voice sounds through the speaker.

I instinctively cringe at her use of *Mrs.* and my married name, but I don't stop to dwell or correct her. The vice principal sounds concerned, and I'm suddenly nauseous. "Is Sasha okay?"

"She's fine, but there was an incident during rehearsal. Sasha tripped over some Christmas lights on the stage and fell on her wrist. It doesn't seem to be broken, but—"

"I'll be right there!" I end the call and turn to my mother. "Sasha fell and hurt her wrist. I need to pick her up."

"Oh, heavens." She looks up to the ceiling as I rush around her. "Go, go. Please call me when you get to Dr. Stevenson's office."

"Of course," I call over my shoulder as I race down the hall toward my purse and keys.

In my car, I check the backseat and find Sasha's *friend*—a stuffed pink elephant. It's the companion she keeps in here. She has a stuffie for the car, her room, the bathroom, and one she keeps in her backpack for school. The latter is her *secret* kitty she never takes out while in class to avoid getting into trouble, but even so, she says it's comforting to know it's with her.

As I drive, I tap my fingers on the steering wheel, my nerves rattled.

Sasha's brave and strong, and the vice principal said

she's okay, but she's my little girl. Anytime tears well in her eyes, my chest squeezes and I want to cry with her.

I've always been protective of her, but I have to admit, since Heath and I split, I've become borderline overbearing as I do everything I can to ensure she doesn't feel neglected or like she's missing out on anything by not having both parents in the same house.

I'm a ball of emotions by the time I reach the school and rush inside toward the auditorium where they hold rehearsals for the Christmas pageant. Muffled noises grow louder once I pull open the doors, and kids in costume chase each other around on stage, jumping over a fallen Frosty and other debris lying about like a tornado whipped through here.

"Sasha? Sasha?" I call out as I hurry down one aisle until I spot her in the front row.

"Mommy!" Sasha stands and brushes past the program director toward me.

My heart soars as I kneel in front of her, studying every inch of my daughter like her life depends on it. In the process, I accidentally grab her arm, which makes her wince. "Oh, I'm so sorry, honey."

Sasha tucks her arm and retreats into herself like a turtle in its shell.

"Let's get you to Dr. Stevenson. He'll fix you up right away," I reassure her and dip my head to look into her eyes. "I bet he has those big candy canes you like too."

Her eyes light up, and a sweet smile teases her thin little lips, putting me at ease. She has her father's smile, and although anything that reminds me of him used to be too painful for me, I'll never associate Sasha with any of the bad.

She's the one thing Heath and I did right.

After I speak with the program director and thank the vice principal, I usher Sasha toward the door and outside to my car that's parked on the side of the street. Thankfully, we didn't take long enough to get a ticket for parking illegally— just what I would've needed.

"Where's Grandma? She promised me we'd make gingerbread cookies." Sasha settles in her seat and struggles with the seatbelt, so I reach in and help her tug it all the way around until I hear the click.

Ignoring the fact that they'd made plans to bake cookies this weekend and not tonight, I smooth her hair to the side. "We'll make them as soon as Dr. Stevenson gets you wrapped up."

"I'm feeling better." She turns her tear-stained face toward me, and my chest tightens.

"I know you're excited to make cookies, but your arm is swollen. We can't leave it untreated, or it'll get worse." I kiss her temple and step back to close the door.

Once I'm behind the wheel, my heart beating at a normal pace, her high-pitched voice sounds again. "I like seeing Grandma Macy so much. She lets me paint her nails and fix her hair. She smells like roses too."

I smile as I turn down a narrow road lined with leafless trees and sidewalks that are sprinkled with white dust. Christmas lights are strung around the limbs and some stoops, adding a cheerful color to the otherwise bleak street. They're celebrating the holidays coming up, and a sense of peace settles in my chest, especially since the tremble isn't as audible in Sasha's voice the more we talk.

I peek at her in the mirror as I say, "Grandma likes hanging out with you too. Remember when she took you to see the tall Christmas tree at Rockefeller Center?"

"Yes!" She claps, then gasps, followed by a loud cry.

"What? What is it?" I glance over my shoulder, then quickly return my focus to the road. "Sasha?"

In a watery voice thick with emotion, she says, "I hurt my wrist again."

"Okay, sweetie, hang in there." I call the doctor once more since his office didn't answer on the way to Sasha's school, but I get a response this time. I exhale with relief and say, "Hi, this is Isabel Michaels." I come to a stop at a red light and again turn to check on Sasha. "I'm bringing my daughter to see Dr. Stevenson. She hurt her wrist at a play rehearsal, and I think it might be sprained."

A woman's voice comes through the Bluetooth speaker. "I'm sorry, but Dr. Stevenson has already left the office for the holiday. I can give you a referral, though, if you'd like."

"Shoot," I mutter under my breath as Sasha lets out a disappointed whimper.

"Ma'am?" the receptionist asks.

"A referral would be great," I relent.

"What? No candy cane?" Sasha asks, panic laced in each word.

"I'll give Dr. Rollins a call. His and Dr. Blythe's offices are located close to ours, and I know Dr. Rollins is accepting new and emergency patients." She rattles off the address, and once we end the call and I'm at another red light, I put it into my maps app.

"No candy cane?" Sasha repeats, her tone still as sad as before.

"Sorry, Sash, but we're going to meet a new doctor. Meeting new people is fun, right?" I glance in the mirror at her to see if she relaxes, but she merely shrugs and clutches the pink elephant in her lap with one arm.

Sighing, I follow the directions given from the app as little white flecks start falling onto the windshield.

"It's snowing!" Sasha squeals like it's the first time she's seeing snow.

I smile as we pull into the new doctor's office. This is my favorite time of year—cold weather, cinnamon everything, and scarves. I have half a closet full of the latter; they're my kryptonite, and I wait all year to be able to show them off.

Today, I'm wearing a crocheted infinity scarf I bought myself last Christmas, and Sasha and my mother agree it's my holiday scarf because of its bright red color and subtle gold accents in the yarn.

Snowflakes stick to my lashes as I round the car to help Sasha out, and I send a quick prayer that this Dr. Rollins keeps the smile on my daughter's face.

But her smile falls as we get out of the snow—she loves this time of year as much as I do—and reach the front desk. Wrapped in my arms, Sasha buries her face in my scarf as I check us in.

"Dr. Rollins is finishing up with a patient and will be right with you and Miss Sasha." The receptionist nods, her eyes warm and kind, immediately settling some of my worry.

I take a seat with Sasha in my lap, nudging her to sit up. "Hey, don't fall asleep yet. We have work to do."

"It feels late," she mumbles, holding her arm.

I scan our surroundings, searching for anything to distract her with. "Want to check out the Christmas tree?" I point to the corner where a green fir stands tall, and the star topper touches the ceiling, tilting to the side.

Sasha rubs her eye and nods.

I set her down, and we walk over to read the homemade ornaments, which seem to have been made by other young patients. It's sweet, really, how many different colored stars cut out from construction paper decorate the tree. A strong pine-like smell infiltrates my senses, and I smile. "A real tree —nice touch," I say under my breath, taking a thin and prickly leaf between my fingers.

"Thanks," a low voice says from behind us. "I love the smell of a real tree. Makes it feel more like Christmas."

I grip Sasha's hand in mine and turn. "I agree. We get one—"

My words get caught in my throat the second I lay eyes on him.

His bright blue eyes.

Easy smile.

Gruff voice.

He's wearing a red-and-white hat, which sits crookedly on his head. His white lab coat is open down the middle, revealing a crisp turquoise dress shirt that makes his eyes pop.

A sexy Santa.

The charming man from the fundraiser.

He's my daughter's new doctor.

## FIVE

## GRAHAM

H oly shit—it's her.

I step forward, my hand outstretched and close to touching her arm, but I catch myself at the last minute and duck down, instead. As I crouch to be eye level with the sweet young girl by her side, the white ball of my Santa hat falls over my eye. When I swipe it away, I notice the girl's hair is the same chestnut color as the woman's, but hers has a tight curl to it. There's also a playful bounce to it that I imagine matches her bubbly personality.

On any other day, anyway.

The girl's eyes are similar to the woman's too. Only, right now, the girl holds fear in them as she clutches her arm close to her chest like it's a security blanket. Briefly glancing at her wrist, I note it doesn't look like a break. There's no deformity, and she idly wiggles her fingers without wincing—a good sign.

But there's swelling, and she's in pain.

I brush aside my shock and mind full of questions, because I have a job to do.

When I smile, it comes out more easily and genuine

than I expected. This little girl is afraid, but she's so adorable and reminds me of Tessa as a child. She broke her arm once, and her tears gutted me worse than the horror I felt at how large her arm had swelled up.

I kneel in front of the woman and girl, resting one knee on the floor and letting Judy's Christmas playlist float above us. My mind is such a mess, I almost forget it's the fourth time today I've heard this particular song. "My name is Graham. What's yours?"

"Sasha," she whispers, peeking at me through the tears brimming in her eyes.

"It's nice to meet you, Sasha." I lean in and use my hand to exaggerate covering my mouth as I say out of one side of it, "And who's the pretty lady with you?"

This earns me a tiny giggle out of the girl. "My mommy. Her name is Isabel."

*Isabel.*

I gulp, risking a glance up to the woman I've spent the last two weeks thinking about—except she's even more stunning than I recall. Her makeup is more natural now than it was at Carter's charity dinner. Her cheeks glow, and a few snowflakes from outside melt in her long hair.

Whether in a floor-length velvet gown or in jeans, boots, and a thick scarf, Isabel is a vision.

She meets my gaze over Sasha's head, her lips parted and eyes full of overwhelming emotions.

*Professional. Be professional.*

Focusing back on my new miniature patient, I hold my hand out for her. "Guess what?"

"What?" She takes my hand, and I lead her and Isabel around Judy's desk to an exam room.

"I have the perfect Christmas cure for your wrist."

She raises her eyebrows, and in my periphery, I can see Isabel's shoulders relax.

"What is it? What is it?" Sasha's lip eases its quiver.

"How do you feel about magic reindeer pills that cure even Rudolph? I ordered them through rush delivery." I wink as I open the door and pat the seat for a giggling Sasha to hop onto. "What do you think?"

"Are they *really* magic?" She tilts her head, and an adorable smile plays across her bright and innocent features.

"Of course." I spread my arms out. "Only the best for my favorite patients."

"But you just met me, silly." She shakes her head, kicking her legs where they dangle over the edge of the bed, then glances at her mom. "I like Grant, Mommy."

I laugh under my breath as Isabel leans over to correct her, "It's *Graham*, sweetie."

My exhale transforms into a strangled gush of air at the sound of my name coming from her lips. She didn't know it the night we met—the night I got to know her body before I learned anything else about her.

I never expected how much I'd like her to say my name.

Or... scream it in private.

*Get a fucking grip, Rollins.*

Wheeling my short stool up to Sasha, I hold my hand out for her wrist. "May I?"

Using my practiced gentleness, I turn her hand over, palm up, and rub my thumb around her wrist. I end with paying special attention to the bone on the side, but it's tender and swollen all over.

Sasha grimaces the whole time I examine her injury and eventually leans her head to the side and into Isabel's stomach.

My heart lurches.

I don't see a ton of kids, but when I do, treating them is the most difficult part of my job. Sometimes, they cry so hard they can't breathe, but the most minute injuries are tough to grapple with too.

"How did this happen?" I ask in an attempt to distract her.

"At rehearsal for the Christmas pageant."

I place her wrist back in her lap. "Oh?"

"I'm a turtle dove." She holds her head high with pride.

I raise an eyebrow. "And you hurt yourself trying to fly?"

"No!" She uses her small free hand to cover her mouth as she lets out a squeal. "I can't fly!"

"Oh, my bad." I shrug.

"Me and Chandler are turtle doves from the 'Twelve Days of Christmas.' Have you heard the song? We sing it at every rehearsal, so I know it really well. I can teach it to you if you want."

Isabel laughs, patting her shoulder. "Let's focus on getting you better, honey. Then we can teach Graham the song." She stiffens like she's surprised she said it—like she didn't mean to involve me any further than this office visit.

The thought would make sense, given how quickly she ran away from me the last time we met, but it stings, nonetheless.

"Do you know what turtle doves mean?" Sasha watches me, her cheeks having lost their rosy tint since getting warm. "They're love. That's why we always see two of them together. And they make this sound—*turrr turrr*. It sounds like *turtle*, and my teacher Mrs. Jarvis says that's why they're called turtle doves." She stops to take a deep breath, still watching me.

"Wow. I didn't know any of that." My lips curl as a slow smile spreads.

"Mrs. Jarvis teaches us a lot." Sasha squirms on the seat as Isabel rubs her back.

"Was she there when you fell?" I ask, feeling Isabel's eyes on me.

Normally, I chat with my patients, make them feel welcomed and distracted from their ailments, and treat them with as minimal discomfort as possible. I don't normally extend their visit longer than necessary, but with Isabel and her daughter, I can't help but want to keep them here just a little while longer.

It's easy to talk with them, even though they're not here under the best of circumstances.

Even though Isabel's sweet perfume is making it difficult not to lean in just a little closer for an extra whiff.

Sitting hunched over her arm, Sasha shakes her head, her hair bouncing back over her shoulders. "I tripped over Christmas lights when Chandler pushed me."

My eyes snap up as Isabel gasps, stepping forward and crossing her arms over her chest. "I didn't know she pushed you."

Sasha shrugs, averting her gaze toward the ground and touching her headband. "She liked my headband, but I wouldn't let her have it."

"We'll talk about this when we get home, okay?" Isabel rubs her upper shoulder, then paces alongside the bed, running both palms down her jean-clad thighs.

She's a good mom. I can tell that by a single visit. She and her daughter are close too. They have an easy and loving dynamic, much like Tessa and our mom have always had.

*Shit.* Why does she have to make me like her even more than I already do?

"What do you think?" Isabel asks me, her voice sweet and velvety like apple cider, albeit laced with concern as she fingers her thick scarf. "Does she need an X-ray?"

Ignoring the small hope that blooms in my chest when I again note the absence of a ring on her finger like I did the last time, I give them a reassuring grin. "Not necessary. Those are no fun, and you, little lady, have a sprain. It's nothing a couple days of rest and ice won't cure."

"And the magic pills!" Sasha quips. "You promised."

"Of course." I wink. "I have another surprise for you too."

"Is it a candy cane?" Her wide eyes light up. "Dr. Stevenson has candy canes, even when it's not Christmas time. I lick them until they turn white!"

I dip my head, chuckling, and I hear Isabel's soft laugh too. It's warm.

And it feels like coming home.

But I know that can't be right.

Before she walked in here, I didn't even know her name, let alone that she has a daughter. The idea that we have something special between us is just that—an idea. It's all in my head.

My nerves on high alert are just because I'm still shocked at seeing her again and haven't yet wrapped my head around it—that's all.

"No candy canes, but how does a Christmas sugar cookie sound?" I manage through the thick lump in my throat, then turn to Isabel and whisper, "Is it okay to give her one?"

"Sure. She can take it home and eat it after we have dinner." Isabel nods, dipping her head until her chin disappears into her circular scarf. It's adorable, and suddenly, I wish I didn't have to let them go.

What're they having for dinner?

What's her number?

Is she free for coffee tomorrow?

All these questions are on the tip of my tongue, desperate to be released, but this isn't the time or the place. I'm at work, and her daughter is staring at me so hard, I'd think I was her favorite cartoon character.

"I'm going to wrap up your wrist, and then we'll get that cookie from Judy. How does that sound?" I ask Sasha and get to work as she tells me more about her play next week— three days before Christmas.

She goes on to describe what toys she asked Santa for and what snack she'd like to leave out for him since "he'll probably be hungry after riding around the world all night on his sleigh," as she says.

Her words are rushed, coming out in what seems like a single breath, all while Isabel steals glances at me, her smile warm. But her eyes reflect something else entirely.

They're at war, and I fight the urge to reach out and touch her—my God, how I want to touch her again. She's back in my life after I thought for sure I'd never see her again, but I can't so much as give her an innocent hug.

Pure torture is what this is.

Once I'm finished, I guide Sasha off the bed, careful not to shake her wrapped wrist too badly.

"Can we see the cookie lady now?" Sasha asks, her demeanor much brighter than when she first walked in. And when she hugs my leg, my heart swells so damn big, I forget how to say a single word.

All I can manage is a nod as I pat her back.

I lead the way for her and Isabel out into the hall, but as

soon as Sasha lays eyes on Judy and the plate of cookies on her desk, she takes off.

"Hey, remember your manners, Sash," Isabel calls out to her as the little girl stops next to Judy's chair, holding her injured arm up to show her.

"She knows how to tug on the heartstrings, that's for sure." I chuckle, my voice low so only Isabel can hear me. "She's an adorable kid."

Isabel places her hand on my arm and stops us several feet away from Judy and Sasha, who's now talking about her costume for the pageant and how big her wings are. "Listen, I'm really sorry to show up like this. If I would've known it was your office, I wouldn't have—" She stops, and the hair on the back of my neck stands.

I follow her bobbing throat as she swallows.

Is her throat as dry as mine?

The pictures of the Hudson River and New York City skylines on the wall beside us blur as I stare into her eyes, trying my damnedest to find... something.

Anything.

"You wouldn't have what? Wouldn't have come?" I tilt my head, noting worry in her expression. Although it's probably for her daughter, it doesn't fucking hurt any less that she implied she wouldn't have come had she known it was me.

She left then, and she'll leave now without a backward glance.

I've gotten a second chance, but nothing's changed. Not for her, anyway.

I turn just as she says, "It's not what you think."

"Funny, because you haven't given me the chance to tell you what I think," I say over my shoulder and continue toward Judy's desk, on the edge of which Sasha sits.

Isabel follows behind me, picks up Sasha, and thanks Judy and me for helping them.

Then, she's gone.

And I let her leave with only the faint scent of her perfume to keep me company.

## SIX

ISABEL

"Can I play in the snow tomorrow? Grandma says we're going to get more." Sasha clutches the cover, pulling it up to her chin. She's up past her bedtime, which rarely happens, but she and Grandma insisted we binge cartoon holiday movies as an impromptu girls' night.

Smiling, I take a seat on the edge of her bed and tuck the blanket in on the other side of her. "We just got you cured from your fall. Now you want to risk getting hurt again so close to Christmas?"

"But I won't get hurt. I took the magic pills, and now, I'm fine." She waves her arm—the one she hurt earlier this week—and shrugs for good measure.

The "magic pills," which were just anti-inflammatory medicine, have worked wonders, I'll admit, and the swelling is nonexistent.

I continue patting the covers down around her as my mind drifts to Dr. Rollins.

*Graham.*

He was good with Sasha—so kind and generous to make her laugh when she was hurting. He made such a significant impression on her that she's asked about "Dr. Santa" several times since her visit.

"If I do get hurt again, Grant will help me get better. He's nice." She nods, her eyes dancing when they should be growing heavier with impending sleep.

My stomach flutters, even though she still gets his name wrong when she's not calling him Dr. Santa. As I smooth my shirt down over my red-and-white pajamas that Sash picked out for me last Christmas, I gently urge, "Honey, you need to go to sleep, okay? You're going to see your father tomorrow for lunch, and then the Christmas pageant is tomorrow night."

"Is Dad coming to the pageant?" She doesn't look at me when she asks, fiddling with her fingernails over the blanket, instead.

Sighing, I swipe wisps of hair from her forehead and kiss her there. "He'll try, baby."

Without another word or protest, she lifts on her side and grabs the stuffed green dinosaur from her nightstand, clutching it to her chest as she settles back into bed.

She presses her eyes closed like she does when she blows out birthday candles, and my heart squeezes.

I was worried about her when Heath and I divorced. I insisted on keeping the house she's grown up in so she'd have some normalcy. My mother hangs around a lot too and ensures Sasha has family close by.

It's helped, but Sasha's relationship with Heath still suffers. When she was a baby, he was close with her. He worked from home as often as he could and prioritized time with her to ensure he didn't miss the milestones.

But she doesn't remember any of that. All Sasha knows are his frequent absences, not only from home now that he's moved out but also from her activities and plays. On occasion, she asks about her father, but her voice never goes up an octave as it normally does when she's excited, like when we go see Christmas lights every year.

Her voice was flat when she asked if her father's coming tomorrow night. In all the chaos of Sasha's accident, dealing with her classmate tripping her, and last-minute shopping, I don't think I've even told Heath that Sasha's in a play. The only thing we've discussed recently is her attendance to an early Christmas lunch hosted by him and his new fling.

I insisted that Sasha not be exposed to his parade of women, but he assured me this one's serious and that I *shouldn't act so jealous.*

If only he knew exactly how I've moved on.

I haven't felt anything romantic for Heath in years, and it certainly hasn't changed now, especially after meeting Graham. It only took a quick and secret encounter in a closet to realize how broken Heath and I were in the years leading up to the end.

The tension in Sasha's brows softens as she drifts off to sleep, and I kiss her temple again. Standing, I grab my phone from her nightstand and leave her room, closing the door behind me as softly as I can manage.

As I make my way down the hall, I send a quick text to Heath about the play and get an immediate response that he'll do his best to attend. It's what I figured he'd say since all of his responses are generally the same.

In the kitchen, my mom bounces around with more energy than I'd expect at this hour—it's past her bedtime too.

I take a seat at the barstool and rest my elbows on the marble counter, my chin falling into the palms of my hands. "What has you so cheery?"

She faces me, a mischievous tilt to her smile. "Sasha is

well and in bed, so it's our turn to party." Holding her hand out like a game show host presenting a prize, she reveals two mugs brimming with small marshmallows.

"Hot chocolate?" I cross my arms, sitting back.

"Yes, hot chocolate, but with my special touch and flair."

"Cinnamon? That's pretty common."

"No. It's brandy." She drops her hands to her sides. "Don't be such a killjoy."

I laugh softly, rubbing my eyes.

"Now, let's drink our spiked hot chocolate and watch the Hallmark holiday romances I saved on your TV earlier." She grabs both mugs and rounds the counter toward the living room, leaving me alone with my mouth hanging open.

"I'm sorry. What just happened?" I slide off my stool and follow her, blinking rapidly. "I thought you were tired?"

"Look, Sasha had the right idea about girls' night. Except we need the adult version, and this is all I could muster on short notice." She raises the mugs, causing the melting marshmallows to slosh across the top. Then, she leans into her hip, raising her chin to the side, and it's obvious her mind is concocting some sort of plan. "Maybe we should watch something a little more adult-like too. Sue told me about an awfully scandalous show on Netflix with hot young men and a wild mother of two."

My jaw drops even lower than before. Who is this person? Because she looks like my mother, but she definitely doesn't sound like her. "No way!" I hiss, suddenly feeling like a teenager when she tried to talk to me about *the birds and the bees*. "Besides, since when does upscale, buttoned-up Sue watch filthy TV?"

Mom waves me off. "The only reason she mentioned it was to criticize women of today, but she only made me want to watch it more. You should too."

"What even... I don't understand..."

"Never mind any of that. Bottom line is that you need some fun. You haven't gone out since the charity event, and I don't even know the last time you went out before then. This isn't going out, but it'll do." She sets our mugs on top of two coasters on the coffee table and holds her finger up. "Be right back."

I watch after her as she shuffles through the archway and into the hall. I'm still staring while she rummages through cabinets, then reappears shortly afterward with a blanket in her arms.

"I've gone out," I say, a rough edge to my tone.

"What you've done is focus on being a mother, and you're a damn good one at that."

I nod, silently thanking her, because it's a big relief to hear it out loud every now and then.

"But you've neglected to be a woman, which all of us mothers need to embrace every now and again." She waves over herself. "I know I need it, and it's been a long time for me too. I'm always *Grandma*, which I love, but I think we both need to kick back tonight."

I chew the inside of my cheek, toying with the hem of my loose pajama shirt.

"Sasha is healthy after that scare with Chandler, the little weasel, and—"

I hold my hand up. "It was an accident."

"That's what she and her greedy mother claim, but I digress." She pins me with her stare. "In any case, Dr. Stevenson worked a miracle and cured our girl, so we should celebrate. Plus, it's Christmas, our favorite time of year."

She spreads her arms around the living room, which is decked in red-and-green décor. Twinkling lights on the tree flicker, casting a soft glow across the space. The rug under the coffee table has reindeer floating across the top, matching the skirt under the tree.

A plate of homemade gingerbread cookies we baked and decorated with Sasha sits on the end table, waiting for Santa to eat them. But my mom and I both agreed we'll eat most of them ourselves by Christmas morning.

Our favorite time of year, indeed.

"Graham—*err*, Dr. Rollins," I correct myself, my cheeks heating. Even saying his name out loud, each syllable sinfully rolling off my tongue, is like feeling his hands on me again.

How possessively his hands roamed over my bare skin, cherishing me.

His kisses made me dizzy, and there was an underlying promise in each swipe of his tongue against mine.

I've regretted running away from him ever since I saw him again. That night, it seemed like the responsible thing to do. But since he treated Sasha, all I've felt has been guilt.

And more regret.

"What?" my mother asks, breaking my spell.

I shake my head. "Dr. Stevenson was out, so we were referred to Dr. Rollins."

"Oh. You didn't mention that."

"I don't mention a lot of things." I drop my hands to my sides, shifting from one foot to the other, suddenly nervous.

She holds her hands up like she's surrendering, her eyes wide and innocent. "All right. I didn't mean anything by it."

"I'm sorry." I frown.

My mother eyes me. "Did you see that wild friend of yours recently?"

"Blair?" I pinch my brows together. "No. Why?"

"She's fun to be around but quite a bit unnerving, if you

ask me. You sometimes get an edge when you've been around her." She shrugs. "What's the matter with you, then?"

"Nothing. Absolutely nothing. I'm just tired." I scratch my forehead, then run my fingers through my hair as I let out a rough exhale. The truth is, I'm losing my mind.

I don't like how I left things with Graham.

He seemed to think I ran away from him that night because I didn't feel anything for him, but that wasn't it at all. Quite the opposite, actually, and the urge to go back to his clinic to explain only grows with each passing day.

I need to see him again.

"What aren't you telling me?" My mother quirks her eyebrow and places one hand on her hip.

I grab a cookie and stuff half of it in my mouth, my heart rate spiking. "I kind of... *know* the new doctor," I whisper around the baked good, small brown flecks flying out from between my lips like the mess that I am.

"Oh?" She draws out the sound, her tone completely changing from concerned and accusatory to pleasantly intrigued.

I've always been close with my mom, but as I've gotten older, we've become even closer, especially after my dad passed and I got divorced. We lean on each other, and our relationship has evolved.

I know when she's taken aback and surprised, and it's evident now.

Some days, though, it feels like we're getting to know each other all over again, and I instantly get a feeling I'm about to see another new side of her.

"And how exactly do you know him?" she asks, her voice a higher octave than before.

"Let's just say, the charity event held plenty of excitement to last me through next year, and not because of Blair. She wasn't even there." I laugh, but it's a nervous, breathy sound that doesn't feel like my own.

But it's one that feels familiar, like my giddy laughter from high school after the first time I held hands with a boy I was crushing on.

*What happened to that girl?*

Instead of answering as I thought she might—something involving morals, reputation, and anything Sue would advise—my mother spreads the fluffy throw blanket over the couch cushions and points to one side. "Sit and tell me everything. Scandalous TV can wait now that we have the real thing."

I bury my face in both hands, my cheeks on fire as I start to tell her about Graham, leaving out the dirty details, of course. No matter how good of a listener she is or how old and mature we are, she's still my *mother*.

"A doctor, huh?" My mother clinks her mug to mine, her lips curling in an impressed smile. "Nice work."

I squeeze my eyes shut and laugh, the blush still hot and obvious on my cheeks.

As we sit and talk while sipping on our now-cold drinks, I start feeling more like myself than I have in a while. Tonight, I'm silly and content, and by the time my head hits the pillow a couple hours later, I'm even more determined to make things right with Graham.

Even if he doesn't forgive me and we don't get a chance to see what we could be outside of a dusty closet, I'll be happy because the brief moments we shared were special and life-changing.

The kind that movies are made of.

The kind I need to fight for.

## SEVEN

## GRAHAM

"Damn it," I mumble under my breath.

"Dr. Rollins," Judy hisses from behind the front desk as I skirt around it, white coat flinging backward like a cape.

"Sorry." I hang my head, coming to a stop and turning my phone screen toward her. "I'm waiting on the final Christmas gifts I ordered last week, and their delivery is delayed until after the holiday."

"You know, if you worked a little less, you would've been able to do your shopping in advance. Or on time, at least." She eyes me over the red rim of her glasses.

"That doesn't help me." I narrow my gaze at her, my lips twitching. She always gives me hell for working too many hours, much like my own mother.

But they don't realize this is my job, one I've worked all my life for, and I'm going to do everything I can to excel at it.

In any case, I've been here at the office more than ever the last few weeks because it's the holiday season, which means flu and cold symptoms run more rampant than last-minute shoppers on Christmas Eve. What am I supposed to do? Let New Yorkers cancel Christmas because of their coughs and stuffy noses? I'm not too much of a joyful holiday fan, but even I can't let that happen.

Not when there's something I can do to help.

"Besides"—I wave around the empty waiting room—"it looks like it's an early evening today, so I'll have plenty of time to race around the city for three more gifts. No problem," I say sarcastically, knowing good and well there's nothing I'd rather do than go for a run, then hole up in my apartment and watch reruns of old sitcoms on TV.

"You better get those presents, Dr. Rollins." Judy points at me. "Especially for that sweet sister of yours. She always gets you something thoughtful, and you forget to get her anything at all, so you grab something from your stash of backups from your apartment for her."

I scoff. "I don't do that."

She crosses her arms, obviously not believing me for a second. "Why don't you get going, and I'll wait for Dr. Blythe to finish with his last patient of the day? I'll lock up afterward."

"I couldn't ask you to do that." I shake my head. "You should go spend time with your family."

"Burt went to visit his wretched sister today, and our son is doing Christmas with his girlfriend tonight. I'm free to lock up."

I exhale, scratching my chin, then give in. "All right, but if you need anything—"

"I know where to find you." She smiles warmly at me and gets back to work on entering new patient files into our database, clicking away on her computer and dismissing me.

Chuckling, I turn to head back to my office when the front door swings open, and a woman rushes inside. The scarf she wears covers most of her face, and I don't blame her—it's cold outside, and the snow is coming down pretty hard. According to my weather app, it's only going to get worse.

"Hello. How can..." My voice trails off as she pulls her scarf down and throws her hood backward, revealing gorgeous chestnut hair and defined cheekbones. "Isabel?"

I jerk forward out of instinct, desperate to hold her—and warm her up. But I stop myself, planting my feet firmly on the ugly tan tile of our floor that I hope to replace after the New Year.

"Hi," she breathes, her shoulders shivering as she seeks refuge for her chin in her woven scarf again.

I work my jaw back and forth, very aware that Judy is staring between us, glasses pushed all the way in place. Her clicking on the keyboard slows, and I gather my wits, stepping forward. "Are you feeling okay? How is Sasha—does she need anything?"

Isabel shakes her head, a warm smile spreading across her beautiful face. "No, nothing like that, but thank you for asking."

"Of course." I still study her, but she seems fine. Plenty of color in her cheeks and clear eyes. When she swallows, she doesn't seem to have any difficulty because of swollen lymph nodes, but I'd have to feel them to be certain. "What can I do for you?" I ask, and it takes every ounce of energy to keep my tone professional.

She takes a deep breath, never removing her gaze from mine. "I'm sorry about the other day. I would really like to explain—I need to. I can hardly sleep or think about anything else, and I'd just appreciate if I could—"

My jaw comes unhinged, and I don't realize I'm leaning forward, waiting for the rest of her sentence like I'm waiting for a diagnosis. But before I can get it, she's cut off by chatter from the other hall as Dr. Blythe and his patient appear at the front desk.

"This time, hold off on cycling until the swelling in that knee goes down, Lance Armstrong." Dr. Blythe chuckles as he pats a short man on the shoulder.

I shake my head at yet another of my partner's terrible jokes. He means well, though, and I respect him for that and many other things.

I flick my gaze back to Isabel, who's pulled her hands from her pockets and smoothed her scarf farther down, giving me a full view of her face. "I want to talk too," I say.

"Oh! I almost forgot," Dr. Blythe's voice booms again, and in my periphery, I see him lean his elbow on the counter at reception as he settles in for a little conversation. Given he's my dad's old partner, I've known him long enough to read his body language, and I can tell he's going to be a minute.

When he asks Judy to grab something out of the office behind reception and she disappears, I take my chance.

Flustered and on edge with anticipation to hear what Isabel has to say, I take her hand in mine and lead her through the nearest open door. I need privacy to talk to this woman who's had me bent out of shape all month.

What is going through her head?

Mind racing, I shut the door behind me, enveloping us in darkness, and immediately, I'm assaulted by the smell of bleach. We spin in place, bumping into each other like we're two leaves in the wind, colliding through no fault of our own.

Feeling along the wall, I find a switch and flip it, bringing a dim light to life overhead. It's not much, but at least when I turn, I can see enough of Isabel's face now.

"This feels strangely familiar." I wipe my hands down my coat, recalling the first night we met.

We'd disappeared into a closet for the best night I've ever shared with a woman, and I didn't even know her name.

She giggles, shuffling from side to side as she takes in our surroundings.

"I swear, it's not on purpose this time," I say. "I just wanted some damn privacy. We have a lot of Chatty Cathys in this office, and Judy is their queen."

"How long has Judy worked here?" She tilts her head, peeking up at me.

Isabel's only a handful of inches away. The tip of my shoe touches that of her boot, and her floral perfume fills every one of my senses, muffling the smell of cleaning products.

"What?" I whisper, my voice dropping several octaves as I already forget the question.

Did I ever even hear the question?

Her eyes roam all over me as she licks her lips, drawing me to the wet sheen she leaves behind, and suddenly, sweat beads down my back. Is it fucking hot in here, or what? "I wanted to talk to you," she says, but her tone isn't as firm or determined like it was before. It's like she's forgotten what she needs to say.

"About what?" I remain still, but when she brings her hand to run through her hair, she barely brushes my arm, which sends my nerves into overdrive.

How am I turned on by a simple fucking brush to my arm? And I'm wearing long sleeves!

"I'm sorry I ran away from you that night." She hangs her head, dropping her gaze to the small space of floor between us. "It's complicated."

"I'm a pretty smart guy." I smirk. "Why don't you explain it to me?"

She worries her bottom lip between her teeth, then pulls her jacket off like she's preparing for a big speech and needs to get comfortable. Her arms flop to her sides as she says, "I'm a divorced mother of a six-year-old. I'm not cool in the slightest and use words like *grumpy*, *dude*, and *kitty headbands* at least twenty times a day. I most certainly don't hook up with random guys I meet at fundraisers, either." She sighs, her shoulders slumping farther forward like she's defeated.

Like any of these revelations could keep me from wanting to be with her.

If only she knew how much this all just makes me want her more.

"So I'm the special exception, then?" I ask as my smile spreads slowly.

"That's right, *dude*." She grins back, swaying in place to an imaginary tune.

Hope blooming in the pit of my stomach, I reach out to tuck a loose strand of hair over her shoulder so I can get a better look at her, but just before my fingers touch her, I drop my hand, along with my smile. "Is that all?"

"I was scared," she blurts. "I still am."

I furrow my brows.

As she inhales, her chest rises, gently kissing the buttons of my dress shirt. She's driving me wild without even trying, but when she speaks up again, her words shaky, my chest sinks. "My divorce was finalized about a year ago, and Sasha has been my priority. She's been my *only* priority, actually, and I've stayed so focused on her and making sure she's transitioning well enough that I forgot how to live, let alone do the whole dating thing." She turns her head to the ceiling, tousling her hair back, and she lets out a humorless laugh. "I was with Heath for ten years. I don't know how to be with anyone else, even if..."

I don't realize I'm staring at her lips until her soft voice trails off. "Even if, what?" I rasp.

"Even if I want to."

The sentence is barely out of her mouth before I place my hands on either side of her face and angle it to the side, planting my lips on hers like I won't get another chance to.

I swallow a happy whimper as her hands weave their way up to my chest, where she fingers the collar of my white coat.

When her lips part, inviting me in, I sweep my tongue inside with languid strokes, enjoying the taste of her.

I *savor* her.

Once we pull back, panting, I lean my head to hers and slide my hands over her shoulders and down to hold her hands between us. "I want to take you out. Get to know you. Hear all about Sasha."

"I'd like that. But first—your number." She grips my hands back, gives them a squeeze, and digs into her pocket. "Shoot. I must've left my phone in the car in my hurry to get inside to see you."

"You were in a hurry?" I grin, and the strain in my pants gets just a little tighter.

She shrugs, obviously trying to appear unaffected, but I know it's an act. Even in the dim light, I can see her blush.

I capture her lips with mine again, but it's a quick and chaste one. "I have mine in my office. Come on. You're not leaving my sight until I get your number this time."

"I'm never going to live that down, am I?"

"Never." I wink, then spin in place to grab the doorknob. Expecting it to open, I'm already walking into the door, but it jams, and I hit my nose against the hard barrier. "What the hell?" I mutter as I try again to throw it open.

But nothing happens.

"What's going on?"

"I don't know," I strain as I continue my feeble attempt at getting it open. Is it cemented shut? *Jesus.* The thing might as well be a vault door at a bank with its locking ability.

The light beneath the door at my feet is dark, and silence surrounds us.

*No, no, no.*

"Judy?" I call out, but I'm answered with more silence.

After a few more pulls, almost dislocating my shoulder, and banging for Judy to open it from the outside to no avail, I sigh, hanging my head. "Well, the good news is that there will be a cleaning crew here around six thirty, which is in"— I yank my sleeve up and check my watch—"an hour."

Isabel's face falls. "I can't wait that long. I need to get to Sasha's play. It's tonight at seven, and she'll be crushed if I'm not there."

"Hey, hey." I rub her upper arms in an attempt to comfort her. "You'll be there. Sometimes, the custodians are early. Maybe today is our lucky day."

She smiles, relaxing in my arms.

And we settle in.

# EIGHT

## ISABEL

"She didn't." Graham brings his hands up to cover his grin, bumping his knees to mine.

As soon as we realized we were stuck in here for what might be an hour, we got comfortable, sitting cross-legged across from each other on the floor and falling into easy conversation.

"She did," I practically squeal. "Sasha asked my mother what *mating for life* means, and she pawned off the answer on me."

His laugh is low and carefree, making me lean in like it's calling to me.

Graham is special—smart, funny, and confident. He's a man who knows what he wants.

When he fisted his hands in my hair and kissed me before, he did it without hesitation or apology, and it was thrilling. It reminded me why the night we met was so remarkable and why I had to come back here today.

We met at random. A moment in time where our worlds collided. And even though there's so much he hasn't told me about himself, at the same time, I know a lot too.

There's always been a familiarity about him—an effortless dynamic that makes me comfortable, yet simultaneously lights me on fire.

The feeling only grows stronger with each passing minute.

"What did you tell Sasha?" Graham asks, placing his hand on my arm, his touch causing heat to run up to my shoulder.

"I didn't say anything yet." My eyes widen in horror of knowing I'll need to eventually address this situation with Sasha. "Thankfully, she has the memory of a typical six-year-old and forgets pretty quickly. She still calls you Grant, by the way. That, or Dr. Santa."

He clutches his chest with one large hand and chuckles. "I'm touched."

I shake my head, smiling. "I mean, what happened to being blissfully unaware at that age? All I cared about back then was what game we'd play at recess or who had the best dessert to trade my orange slices with at lunch. Or what silly crushes the girls and I had. Of course, we were after the same boy all the time." I roll my eyes.

"Oh? And what was this boy like?" Graham rubs his hands together like this is juicy gossip.

"He was *so* great at basketball, and he slid down the red slide the fastest out of all of us," I say, batting my eyelashes and playing along.

"Why, oh why, didn't you marry this stud?"

"We all wanted to, but he chose my friend Kiersten Green. Wrote a poem for her and everything. I wish I could remember it..." I tap my chin, racking my brain.

"Please, for the love of God, remember. I have got to hear this."

"Oh! It went something like: *Roses are red, violets are blue. Please don't be mean, be mine, Kiersten Green.*"

Graham fights a smile and slow claps. "My new damn hero."

I throw my head back and laugh, the sound echoing in this cramped space.

We're stuck together in a small broom closet, and yet, I'm enjoying myself. I shouldn't be surprised, though.

I'm with Graham.

He has this way of putting me at ease but also igniting a deep desire inside me each time he squeezes my hand or sneaks a kiss. It's like he can't keep his hands or mouth off me, and all I can think about is how I want more.

That date he promised can't come soon enough.

"I'll need to talk to Sasha at some point," I say. "But until the time comes, I need to convince her we don't need two pet birds. She asked for them because she's a turtle dove in the play tonight and has become rather enamored by birds now."

He scrunches his nose. "That sounds... fun?" His voice squeaks at the end, and it makes me laugh.

"Exactly what I'm thinking." I sigh, then dip my head to the side. "It's better than wanting a giraffe for the backyard, I suppose."

"You wanted a giraffe?" Graham watches me with a sparkle in his eyes.

I nod. "And my mother told me I couldn't have one because we didn't know how to take care of one. That if we brought one home, it would be sad and cry every day without a big open field to live in, and it would die."

"Ouch. True, but pretty harsh. How old were you?"

"Seven." I laugh, recalling my mother's firm tone all those years ago. She didn't sugarcoat much back then, either. "But I think I'll take a lighter approach with Sasha about the birds. They should be left to fly freely and not trapped in a cage, but I need to say it in a way that doesn't scare her from ever wanting to visit a zoo or something."

He dips his head and chuckles, and it's becoming my new favorite sound. My chest swells as I internally hope to hear it often—if we ever get out of this closet.

"My sister Tessa used to pick the roses from my mother's bushes and stomp on them, as kids do, so one day, she told Tessa that if a thorn from her rose bushes nicked her, she wouldn't grow any taller." He rubs a hand over his forehead, deep in thought. "My mom felt so bad and guilty, she came clean practically in the same breath."

I smile, enjoying each new piece of information I get about Graham and his family. I want to know everything about him.

Sitting this close to him for so long makes me ache too with a desperate desire for him to touch me again like he did that first night.

Clearing my throat to work past the onslaught of heated memories, I manage, "Glad to see I'm not the only one who constantly feels guilty telling my daughter no, even though it's often the right call."

Graham grips my hand, and his tone is serious when he says, "You're doing great. Just like my mom and yours, you're human too, and no one has all the correct answers. You just do your best, and the kids will be better for it. I imagine it's easier said than done, but I'm the kind of guy who talks big so just nod and agree," he teases, chuckling.

I nod up and down, exaggerating my reaction, which makes him laugh harder.

Knowing more about him now, I can tell he's more than

big talk. More than empty words and promises. It makes him even more attractive.

As his expression transforms and shoulders shake, my heart flutters, and I blurt, "Do you want kids?"

He snaps his gaze to mine and instantly sobers again.

I squeeze my eyes closed and wave my hand between us. "That sounded really forward, but I'm simply curious. I'm not one of those crazed women who has kids named after one conversation, and you don't have to answer. I'm—"

"I want kids," he says without a trace of hesitation. "They've always been part of my *someday* plan."

Ease and comfort replace my humiliation.

We stare at each other for a moment, sitting in electrifying silence before I finally manage to swallow and wet my dry throat enough to ask, "How is your sister? And Carter— have you forgiven him yet?"

"I have, although I'm still giving him shit." He breaks his intense focus on me and gives a crooked grin, scratching his chin like he's timid. "Truthfully, I'm starting to be angrier at him for finding *the one* before me. He was always the guy who swore he'd never settle down, and now that he is, I've been feeling like..." He turns his face up toward the ceiling, letting a small laugh loose. "I was going to say I'm feeling like a loser, but I know this is all my pride talking. Didn't realize I was so prideful until Carter so kindly pointed it out a couple weeks ago."

"That must've made you feel even better, coming from him in particular," I joke, my heart doing backflips for this man.

Contrary to his confession, he's not letting any pride get in the way of being vulnerable and real with me right now, and it's making me want him even more.

I didn't think it was possible so soon, but I *want* this man in every way.

His eyes lock on mine, and when he speaks again, his voice is gravelly and full of emotion. "I just want what my parents have. A love that withstands all odds, time, and differences."

I gulp around the swelling lump in my throat. "I know what you mean," I whisper, wholeheartedly agreeing with him, and then, I dip my head as I release a difficult confession of my own. "I thought I'd found it once. I was so sure that Heath was it for me and that we'd be happy and grow old together."

"What happened? If you don't mind me asking."

I glance up. The light illuminates only half his face, but it's enough for me to note the crease between his brows. "His priorities changed. He got the fancy job of his dreams, rented an apartment in the city because he claimed it was more convenient than our house three trains away, and decided he liked the fast pace and excitement of Manhattan more than our quiet life at home. Sasha's first steps and learning her alphabet became less significant somewhere along the way, and well..." I take a deep breath, steadying my voice. "Well, here we are."

I slump, offering a small smile. Not because I'm still sad about the end of my marriage, but because I always get overwhelmed when I think about Sasha and how she won't grow up with her father under the same roof.

But I can't deny how much better it'll be for her in the future. How beneficial it'll be for her to have two happy parents, even if it means they're not together.

Graham pulls my hand in his, his fingers gliding ever so softly across my knuckles. Turning my palm up, he brings it to his lips and places a gentle kiss there, then trails his mouth up to my wrist, where he places another kiss.

It's sweet and sensual and everything in between.

"I'm sorry."

"It's better this way for everyone involved," I whisper, meaning every word.

"You're very strong and unlike any woman I've met."

"What kinds of women have you met?" I quirk a brow, my curiosity piqued.

He chuckles, scratching the back of his head. "Not the right kind, to say the least. One woman I dated was obsessed with my sister. She stole her clothes but claimed she was just borrowing them. Without Tessa's permission, by the way. Another screamed children's rhymes in her sleep *and* when she was angry—I never figured out the correlation between the two. Oh! And the real winner"—he snaps his fingers—"was the woman who very blatantly hit on my father during a family dinner. I should've known better than to invite her, especially since she asked way too many questions about my dad for the week leading up to the dinner," he says animatedly.

"So, what you're saying, Dr. Rollins, is you have poor judgment," I tease.

"Call me *doctor* again. That was hot." He winks, and there's a light tone to his voice, which makes my knees weak. "But if you're wondering if I'm grouping you with the rest of them, you're dead wrong."

"I wasn't..." I gulp, and the rest of my sentence hangs in the air.

The amused glimmer in his eyes is slowly replaced by something else—a longing.

My heart thumps louder in my ears the longer he stares at me like that.

His nostrils flare, and his gaze falls to my parted lips as he says, "It's funny. I wasn't even supposed to be here the evening you brought Sasha in. I was supposed to be at one of Carter's volunteer events."

"Christmas Wrap-Up?" I freeze as I connect the dots of fate in my head.

"Yeah. How did you know?" His eyes, full of shock and wonder, flicker up to search mine.

"I was supposed to be there too. I had plans to take Sasha and make it the start of an annual tradition." I lick my lips.

"Family traditions are important. I want to make those in the future."

"Someone out there wants us to be together," I say, my tone a mix of amusement but also undeniable awe.

Goose bumps erupt along my arms, and my breath catches as he leans in. When he kisses me this time, it's unlike the chaste ones he's given me while we've sat on the floor of this small closet.

This kiss is firm.

Heady.

He delves his tongue between my parted lips and cups my face in both hands, his kiss slow and deliberate. We tangle our tongues together, passion infused in each swipe, stroke, and moan.

I sag forward, leaning into this kiss with everything I have to give.

Without breaking our fused mouths, I continue toward him, rising onto my knees and straddling his waist. I run my hands through his hair as I grow frantic, my blood hot and core tingling.

"God, you taste good," he growls, his words and tone reverberating against the roof of my mouth and causing shivers down my spine.

I hum, grinding my hips into him and rubbing my chest

against his, reveling in how my sensitive nipples cause a new round of shivers to rack through me. "I want you, Graham. I just..." The plea is lodged in my throat as we continue making out like teenagers playing a game of Seven Minutes in Heaven.

This is my heaven.

He curses under his breath. "I don't have any condoms."

Disappointment starts to seep in, but before it consumes me, Graham smiles against my lips. "I have an idea, though." He squeezes my ass in both hands, hoists me up, and brings one hand between us to the button of my jeans.

"Yes," I pant as the sound of my zipper being undone echoes between us.

He dips his hand down my lower stomach and inside my pants until one finger traces the top of my panties, and my mouth falls open.

Desire pools between my legs.

Anticipation races through my veins.

Here, in the dimness of a closet with only a mop and spray bottles of cleaner as witnesses, my senses are heightened, feeling everything Graham does to me quadrupled.

His thumb skates over my belly button as one expert finger slips inside my panties and finds the spot between my legs, the aching in my core intensifying with each passing second that he doesn't touch me where I need him.

"Graham, please," I press, urging him to relieve the need bundled in my lower stomach.

He bites his lip as he drops his gaze between us, where his hand disappears down my jeans.

And then, I feel it.

His finger dipping inside me.

The immediate sensation.

My pulsing desire being satisfied with each stroke and

curling of his hand.

He adds a second finger and uses his thumb to rub circles on the tight bundle of nerves that are screaming with lust.

"Oh, yes," I moan and capture his lips again, feasting on the taste of him as he pumps his fingers in and out of me.

Graham takes his time, working me into a frenzy so dizzying, my vision blurs.

When my head lulls to the side, he cups my cheek and lifts me to face him. "I want to watch you come undone for me, Isabel," he whispers, his voice gruff and sexy as it reaches inside and spurs my body higher.

I nod, breathing his name over and over again, the faint sound quicker as he picks up the pace.

Until I explode in a mix of moans and satisfied pants, my body quivering on top of him as my legs squeeze the outsides of his thighs, then loosen as I fall slack against him.

Wrapping both arms around me, he catches me and tightens his hold in a way that makes my heart so full, it might burst.

How can someone I just met feel so right?

Swallowing past the lump in my throat, I open my mouth to say something when I catch flickers of light beneath the door, followed by muffled voices.

"I think the custodians are here." I tap Graham's shoulder and scramble to stand up, bringing my coat from the floor with me and using it as a shield while I zip my pants back up.

He stands too, his chest brushing against mine as he straightens to his full height. Is his heart beating as wildly as mine?

When can I see him again?

I don't have time to ask before the door is yanked open,

and a blinding light blasts toward us like a laser.

"Dr. Rollins?" A man shorter than Graham glances between us. "This door has been so finicky this week and gets jammed easily. My guy is coming to take a look after the holidays. Are you two okay?"

Graham looks over his shoulder at me, sneaking his hand down to grasp mine, and smiles. "Never better."

We thank him and rush out of the closet, my cheeks flushed and redder than Santa's hat, I'm sure.

"That was a close one," I whisper to Graham as we make our way to the lobby.

My hand is almost on the door when he spins me around to face him and plants a kiss to my mouth, one that holds more promise than if he would've written it across the sky.

It leaves me breathless.

"When can I see you again?" Graham asks, still nipping at my lips as the corners of his own tug upward.

I pull back and grin, gripping his hands. "Come with me to Sasha's play, and we can talk afterward."

"No more closets, though, right?" he teases.

I burst into giggles, feeling my blush deepen. "No. No more closets for us."

"Good because I'm starting to be turned on by brooms and mops, and that's just unhealthy." He shakes his head, intertwining his fingers through mine, and warmth shoots up my arm. "But if I had to be stuck in a closet at Christmas with someone, I'd choose you over and over again."

I release a watery exhale, and my gaze locks onto Graham's as I'm swept up into the deep blue of his mesmerizing eyes. Since words fail me, I lean onto my tiptoes, weave my fingers around his neck, and kiss him, more than glad to have been stuck with him as well.

## NINE

## GRAHAM

As the last note hangs in the air, I lean back in my seat, my hand still on Isabel's thigh because I can't stop myself from touching her.

Children dressed in six different kinds of birds and other costumes flit across the stage, and a handful of tiny drummers are spread across the back of them. A few kids leap in front as girls dance to the side. They're all out of sync, out of tune, and giggling, and it's pretty damn adorable.

Right in the middle of the chaos is Sasha wearing wings larger than her body and an even bigger grin.

Isabel's eyes have remained transfixed on her the entire time. While I, too, am proud of Sasha for getting up there in front of all these people to sing and dance, I'm in awe of her mother as well.

She has a pure heart and wants the wholesome family like I do.

It makes me like her even more, although *like* isn't a strong enough word.

Sasha waves to us in the third row, then disappears behind the pulled curtains.

Isabel wipes at the corner of her eye. "God, I'm a blubbering mess. I just knew I would do this, even though I told myself not to. It's just a play, right?"

"A play that your daughter is in," her mother exclaims from the other side of her as she stands with the rest of the crowd to clap and cheer. "Your *six*-year-old daughter. I can't believe how big she looks up there!"

I join them, grinning from ear to ear as we give a standing ovation as much to the children as well as to the program directors for helping them put this show on.

I came into Isabel and Sasha's lives so quickly, and it's only been a handful of weeks. Yet, they feel like home already.

They feel like the answer to what I've been searching for.

The twinge in my chest that I felt at my parents' house a couple weeks ago was relieved the moment Isabel walked back into my life.

Being locked in a closet with her earlier only helped matters.

There's something deep and meaningful between us, and it's taken two closet encounters to succumb to it. I'm more than ready to see who we are out here in the real world, though, because I know it'll only be better.

And I'm wildly impatient for it.

Once the crowd settles down and we take our seats again, Isabel's mother leans over her lap to extend a hand toward me. Isabel and I rushed in as the first song started, so we didn't get a chance to introduce ourselves. "Now, might you be the doctor my daughter has been daydreaming about for weeks?"

I lift an eyebrow, fighting a smirk as I clutch her mother's hand in mine. "I'd like to hear more about that, please."

Isabel groans, burying her face in both hands. "Don't make me regret bringing both of you, okay?"

"Like there's anything you could've done to make me miss this. Sasha was the star of the show." She withdraws her hand and settles back into her seat, head lifted high with pride for her granddaughter.

"They're kids. They were all cute, and the whole play was sweet." Isabel's lips curl like she's keeping a secret. "But Sash was great."

We each chuckle, agreeing all the same.

"I'm Macy, by the way."

Isabel melts her back into the seat to let her mother introduce herself properly, and I do the same, offering her my best smile in hopes it'll win me some points.

I want to make a good impression on Isabel's family, especially since I'm crashing Sasha's play. It's not lost on me that her own father didn't show up, but no matter how much that angers me for the little girl's sake, it's not my place to voice my thoughts, either.

Sasha emerges from behind the curtains and bounces down the steps toward us, her smile bright and infectious. The ladies skirt past me, and Isabel scoops her daughter up, showering her with praises on her dancing, singing, and costume, which she's still wearing.

I stand beside them to let them have a special moment, stuffing my hands into my pockets and chuckling.

Once Isabel sets her down, Sasha spins in place to show off her costume, twirling like a ballerina and still smiling like this is Christmas morning as Isabel and Macy *ooh* and *ahh*.

Eventually, Sasha spots me, and her eyes widen as she skips toward me like the lords a-leaping earlier. "Graham!

What're you doing here?" She squeals, hugging my leg as Isabel and Macy stand together, peering at us.

The right use of my name instead of *Grant* makes my chest swell with pride that she remembers.

I squat onto the balls of my feet and meet Sasha at eye level. "Your mom invited me, and might I just say, you were the best turtle dove I've ever seen."

She dips her head, swaying from side to side, then holds her arm up. "I'm all better—look!"

"I see the magic pills worked, huh?"

She nods, giggling.

Isabel joins us, kneeling on the other side of her as the auditorium grows louder with all the chatter from the other excited kids and their parents. "How about we get some hot chocolate on the way home?" she asks, giving Sasha's shoulder a little shake.

"Yes! Can Graham come too? Please, please." Sasha holds her hands up in a begging manner. Coupled with her wings, she looks like a tiny angel.

"We'll have to ask him," Isabel whispers, but it's loud enough for me to hear.

Sasha whirls around to me and squeezes my hand in her little one. "Please, Graham, come with us to get hot chocolate! Mommy knows the best place where they put different colors of *marsh-a-mallows* on top and a ton of whipped cream if you want."

"There's nothing else I'd rather do," I say.

"Yes!" She turns to her mom, fist in the air, and announces, "He said *yes*, Mom. Let's go."

Isabel glances at her mother, who's smiling widely. "Coming?"

"No, you three go ahead. I have... a..." She snaps her

fingers. "I have charcuterie night with Sue. But you kids have fun."

"Charcuterie night? That's the best you can come up with?" Isabel asks, accusation laced in each syllable, which makes my lips twitch.

Macy kisses Isabel's cheek, winks at me, then bends down to give Sasha a hug and one last round of praise on her performance tonight.

We make our way toward the door all together with Sasha between Isabel and me. As we maneuver through the crowded aisle, Sasha asks us to swing her, but there are too many other people.

"We can swing you once we get outside," Isabel suggests as we emerge out into the lobby of the school.

Macy waves goodbye, and Sasha stops us by the window, through which the gusts of wind ruffle the tops of the blades of grass outside.

"Daddy isn't here," Sasha says, but it's more of a statement than a question.

My heart sinks as Isabel bends down and turns Sasha toward her. "I'm sorry, honey, but he's working. He's excited to see you tomorrow to open Christmas presents, though. Won't that be fun?"

She nods, a small smile tugging at her lips, and it loosens the knots in my stomach a fraction, especially because Isabel is so good and smooth at replacing Sasha's sadness with happiness.

I don't know how she does it, but Isabel is so strong for the both of them. It's admirable, to say the least, and it makes me want to witness more of it and their bond.

It's pure and beautiful.

At the car, Isabel removes Sasha's wings before setting

her inside, much to her protest, but Isabel eventually wins. Turns out, hot chocolate is more important than a costume.

On the way, Sasha moves on to talking about her pink elephant, gushing over her friend Chandler's Disney-themed birthday party in a couple weeks, and trying to count the snowflakes falling on the windshield.

"And seventy-hundred-thirty," she says matter-of-factly from the backseat, making us laugh.

Instinctively, I reach over the console for Isabel's hand and rub my thumb over her knuckle, content to be here with them.

This all feels oddly, yet comfortably, natural.

A few minutes later, we come to a stop in front of a quaint and cozy ice cream shoppe, complete with multi-colored lights hanging from the wooden awning out front. The small porch underneath holds two tables, and the windows are decorated with canned snow spray, wishing their customers happy holidays.

Isabel rounds the car to Sasha's side. "Here, let me bundle your coat up. And you need to wear your hood, honey."

"I like the snow, though. It tastes good."

"This hot chocolate will taste better if your tongue isn't numb and frozen," Isabel retorts.

"You're so smart, Mommy."

Once Sasha hops onto the ground by the car, she holds her hand out for me, and I resume my position on the other side of her. "You're my mom's new boyfriend, aren't you?" She looks up at me, her eyes filled with reflections from the glowing lights of the ice cream shoppe.

I choke on my own spit, letting out a strangled string of incoherent sounds. What do I say to that?

Isabel dips her head, and I bet if I could see her full face, I'd see a cute blush spreading across her cheeks.

Sasha doesn't let me answer as we make our way to the front door, in the center of which hangs a note that boasts of their hot chocolate—a holiday special they serve for a limited time. "You're her turtle dove. Did you know they're symbols of love and loyalty? Or that they mate for life?" Sasha continues, her head bobbing as she skips to the back of the line to order.

Isabel meets my gaze over Sasha's hair, her cheeks glowing as she smiles, and I can tell she's thinking the same.

That the answer to Sasha's question is yes, and when I get Isabel alone later, I'm going to make it known so there's no confusion.

We may not have been on a proper date yet.

I don't even know her favorite meal, where she and Sasha like to vacation, or how Isabel envisions her next five years, but I know what I want.

As the three of us accept our hot chocolate and laugh over the whipped cream mustache covering Sasha's top lip, I know our traditions are in the making for a long time to come.

We're still creating our history, but I'm certain this woman and her daughter are my future.

## EPILOGUE

### GRAHAM

*Next Christmas...*

Carter chases a squealing Sasha through my parents' living room, and I chuckle, unable to decide which one of them is the bigger kid. They make it around the couch where Carter leans over, clutching his side. "Break—let's take a break."

Shrugging, Sasha opens the door to the kitchen and asks the ladies, "Are you eating all the gingerbread cookies without me?"

With a glass of whiskey in hand, I join Carter on the couch as the women's bubbly chatter drifts toward us, making the corners of my eyes crinkle as a smile spreads.

I take a sip of the burning liquid and tap my foot to the floor, losing myself in the presents under the tree. There's one special present this year that awaits Isabel and me back at our place, and I can't wait to—

"What's that dopey look for?" Carter smacks my shoulder, causing the whiskey in my glass to slosh and a drop to fall onto my jeans.

"What the hell, man?" I groan, leaning forward to set my drink on a coaster and out of harm's way. When I turn back to him to insult his hair or the stupid Christmas sweater Tessa bought for him, I pause, then grin—nothing will ruin my good mood.

"Holy shit," Carter whispers, sitting on the edge of the couch and facing me. "You're going to do it tonight. You're going to pop the question like a sexy Santa pops a wheely in his sleigh."

"What does that even mean?" I throw my head back and laugh, then glance around to make sure Sasha and Isabel are still out of earshot—due to language for the former and the proposal for the latter.

Although it's more of a proposal to both of them.

"It's impossible for a sleigh to do that. I also didn't think it'd be possible for you to settle down. I mean, haven't your mom and her friends been trying to set you up for years before Isabel?"

I nod, a smile teasing my lips. It's one I think will be permanently plastered to my face if Isabel agrees to marry me. Clapping Carter's shoulder, I muse, "The key words there, my wealthy and obnoxious friend, are *before Isabel*."

"Oh, God, don't tell me being in love has turned you into some kind of poet who has a new appreciation for life or some shit. Because if so, we do not have enough whiskey for that." He rolls his eyes as he points to the half-empty bottle on the bar behind us.

"You're one to talk." I stare pointedly at him as I take a drink.

He smooths his palms over the ridiculous sweater he's wearing, cutting his eyes toward the kitchen door behind which Tessa is. "You're right," he says, his voice now serious. "The second Tessa said yes, a whole new life opened up for me. One I didn't think I'd ever have."

I recall the day he proposed to my sister and swallow my sip around the sudden lump in my throat—I know the exact feeling.

No matter how badly I've wanted a family, I didn't think it was in the cards for me. I was dating all the wrong women, but in hindsight, I was seeking them out because I didn't want anyone or anything to interfere with my practice.

Isabel and Sasha are showing me I can have both.

And more.

I've nailed down a stricter schedule that I'm sticking to and not finding excuses to add more to my plate. This way, I'm home for dinner and in time to tuck Sasha in. On the weekends, we have park days, picnics, and movie nights with overflowing buckets of popcorn, all huddled underneath one giant blanket.

Isabel even helped me get organized and prepared so that my family receives considerate gifts on time for Christmas this year. There will be no need to dig into my backup stash, and I suspect I'll never need it going forward.

Sasha's father even comes around more often lately, having realized he's missing out on her growing up. Perhaps it's a legitimate regret, or the presence of another man around that's made Heath be more proactive, but in any case, I'm happy for Sasha's sake.

And when we have the house to ourselves, Isabel and I

definitely use it to our advantage to have romantic date nights that end in heated moments in bed and *elsewhere*.

The shower might be my favorite place—there's something particularly sexy about rubbing my woman down with lavender soap that instantly makes me come alive.

She and Sasha are making me see that things work out when it's meant to be, and the three of us? We're meant to be. This last year with them has been better than I ever imagined. It's the kind of love that makes me almost forget my life before them.

And I want it to last forever.

Carter nudges me, pulling me out of this daze I've been under all evening. "You're always trying to be like me. First, I find *the one*, and you go out and do the same. Then, I propose, and here you are, doing the same. I know I've always been a role model, but isn't this a little much?"

I turn my head to the ceiling. "Why? Why couldn't my sister be engaged to anyone else? Literally, she could've had any other dude."

His palm engulfs my shoulder, and he gives it a shake, his smirk prominent in my periphery. "But that would be so boring, don't you think?"

Chuckling, I agree. The truth is, I'm glad he and Tessa got together. They've been good for each other, and I have to admit, I wouldn't have it any other way.

My dad descends the steps behind us, patting his stomach. "Jesus, those women are trying to kill me. I'm stuffed." He meets my gaze and asks, "Where did Isabel learn to cook like that? Her broccoli casserole tasted like it was made by angels. I'm not going to lie—I almost didn't even want to try it. Broccoli and I aren't the best of friends, but damn. I about ate the whole dish."

"I know." I stand to face him, glaring. "At one point, I almost lost a finger."

He shrugs and waves me off, then pours himself a whiskey.

"Did I hear compliments for the chefs, and we're missing it?" my mother asks, emerging from the kitchen with Tessa, Macy, Isabel, and Sasha in tow.

Sasha has a white substance caked in the corners of her mouth, and immediately, I know she's raided the gingerbread cookies. They're her kryptonite. There aren't enough of them in the world to appease her.

Which makes me smile until I realize the sugar will likely keep her up all night. The last time we picked her up from Macy's in this condition, Isabel and I ended up drinking coffee at midnight while a Disney movie played and Sasha ran around the living room singing tunes from a different movie.

It's hard not to enjoy and admire her zest and energy, though.

I kneel down in front of Sasha. "How many cookies did you have this time?"

"Grandma One gave me two, and Grandma Two gave me two more." She flashes a victorious grin, and I still chuckle at the way she's numbered her grandmas. Including Heath's, she has three, and she thought it'd be fun to number them.

"They didn't know you already had one at the house before we came, did they?"

She shakes her head slowly, narrowing her gaze like the sneaky—and smart—kid she is.

"All right." Macy claps. "I need to get home and to bed if I have any hopes of making it to our yoga class in the morning." She gives my mom a hug, and they finalize plans for her to pick Macy up on the way to the yoga class they started taking together a few months ago.

Yet another activity my mother's taken up during her retirement.

"Sasha needs to go to bed too, although I'm not sure the sugar agrees." Isabel places both hands on her hips and glares at the culprits, who shrug in sync.

Shaking my head, I grab our coats from the closet by the door, where Sasha spins in circles. When she stops, she stumbles to the side and erupts into giggles.

And so, it begins.

"Merry Christmas, everyone." We wave over our shoulders as we nudge Sasha out the door.

She squeals and laughs and talks to her pink elephant the entire ride home as Isabel and I hold hands across the console. It's how we always drive when we're in the car, and I even miss it when she's not here.

If I've learned anything of my parents' relationship of over forty years, it's that the little things matter. Traditions matter. And I plan to keep it all intact and add more with these girls.

*My* girls.

"Oh"—Isabel turns toward me—"I know we haven't even opened Christmas presents yet, but for our romantic summer getaway, what do you think about Dogwood Cove? It's a quaint Canadian town, and they have the Summer Solstice Festival every year. It lines up for when Sasha will be at camp, so it'll be just you, me, and cinnamon sugar BeaverTails." She wiggles her eyebrows.

"Okay, but first—what is a BeaverTail?" I ask skeptically, keeping my eyes on the road.

"Giant pieces of fried dough—aka *heaven*." She sighs dreamily.

"Sounds like a plan, then." I kiss the back of her hand, elated with how she always plans for the future like this. I thought I was usually prepared, but it's nothing like Isabel.

During the last few minutes of the drive, we discuss plans for the big summer trip to the beach for all three of us. We went last summer, and it was a hit, especially with Sasha, so we decided to make it an annual thing.

At the house, my nerves are shot like I'm the one who inhaled several holiday cookies. Unable to wait any longer without putting a ring on Isabel's finger, I move straight to the lit-up tree by the decorated fireplace. Moving aside the large ornament Sasha made when I asked her to help with a secret mission of hiding her mother's Christmas present, I retrieve the small box.

"Sasha, it's getting late. Go upstairs and brush your—" Isabel stops when she enters the living room, coat halfway down her arms, mouth agape.

Sasha slides in from behind her, a big smile on her face as she sidles up next to me.

I'm on one knee.

Heart full.

Emotion clogged in my throat.

"I can't wait until morning." I shift to face both of them and say, "Last year, I spent the couple nights before Christmas stuck in a closet with a woman I'd never thought I'd see again." I eye Isabel and recall the night she showed up at my office, reveling in how much has changed since then. "It was the best holiday I'd had, and it wasn't because of the new computers or office chair we put in at the clinic, but because I met you two." I smile.

Giggling, Sasha sways her hips, and Isabel clutches her chest, tears building in her eyes.

I take Sasha's little hand in mine. "Sasha, you've taught

me so much about Disney's Descendants and how to braid hair, but more than that, you've taught me a love I've never known. I won't replace your father, but I'll always aim to earn and hold a place in your heart because you're in mine." I turn to Isabel and deeply inhale. "Isabel, I'm in love with you because of your heart. Your loyalty. Your laugh. And for many more reasons than there is enough time on Earth to name, and I'll continue trying to be worthy of you, if you'll have me." My gaze bounces between them. "Will you marry me?"

Isabel's cheeks split into a bright and watery smile. Squatting down so that we're all at eye level, she asks, "What do you think, Sash?"

She surprises us both when she shrugs. "I like Grant."

Isabel opens her mouth, horror in her eyes, and I sit back on my heel, speechless.

Then, Sasha breaks into a toothy grin. "Kidding!" She jumps into my embrace and wraps her tiny arms around my neck, her high-pitched laugh better than any music I've ever heard.

Isabel joins us in a group hug as they both cheer and chant, "We're getting married!"

They tackle me to the ground, and I lie here by the Christmas tree, counting my blessings.

Starting with my girls and our future together.

## THE END

Want more of Graham, Isabel, and Sasha?
Grab a FREE Bonus Epilogue here -
https://bit.ly/SACBonus

# 12 DAYS OF KISSMAS

Pine-ing for the perfect holiday romance? It's love at frost sight with The 12 Days of Kissmas! A dozen standalone holiday novellas so steamy they're sure to melt that winter chill. From dashing doctors to dirty-talking mountain men, staying off the naughty list just got a whole lot harder.

Order the whole series on Amazon - https://geni.us/12DaysOfKissmas

Lumber Snack by Mae Harden

Stuck at Christmas by Georgia Coffman

A Christmas Tart by Lola West

Merry Christ-Mess by Dee Ellis

A Very Pierced Christmas by Ember Davis

Delay of Game by Evie Graham

Hot Mess Christmas Express by Claire Hastings

Secrets and Mistletoe by Julia Jarrett

Off the Market at Christmas by Chelle Sloan

Bachelor #10 by Kat Baxter

Under the Thistle-toe by Mindy McKinley

Must Have Been the Mistletoe by M.L. Broome

## ALSO BY GEORGIA COFFMAN

# STUCK WITH THE BILLIONAIRE EXCERPT

## TESSA

*Is Manhattan's Most Eligible Bachelor Finally Settling Down?*

*Spotted (Again): Carter Fields with Supermodel Ginger Myers.*

*Fields's Ferrari vs. a Mailbox. Who won?*

Scoffing, I lean against the wall of the café, my attention glued to my phone while the morning bustle gets going. I keep scrolling the numerous articles, scanning headlines that range from humorous to truly ridiculous. How is Graham friends with this joke?

He's been friends with Carter since college—for fifteen years—and I've never met him. For some unholy reason, my brother Graham thinks inviting Carter to the cabin for my birthday celebration would be the best time to introduce us.

It's supposed to be family only, as it's been in the past.

"Tessa?"

I lift my head at the sound of my name coming from behind the counter and find the barista holding up a drink —my salvation.

As expected, the noisy couple next door kept me awake until long after two in the morning. Their constant moans and pants sounded like they had five people in the room for a giant orgy.

I wanted to barf.

My mouth waters as I push my thick-framed glasses up higher on my nose and make my way to the front for my much-needed drink. I woke up long before my alarm—a treacherous habit—and had two cups of coffee in my apartment to nurse my hangover.

But they weren't enough to soothe me awake from my eighth sleepless night in a row, nor were they infused with the uniquely rich and bold flavor of an espresso shot like this.

I reach the counter as the barista calls my name a second time and slides my coffee forward. My latte in hand, I skirt around the newly formed line and pull my phone back out.

The image at the top is much like the others: clean-cut billionaire Carter Fields in an expensive, well-tailored suit from some designer I'm too inferior to know, a matching shiny watch, and a blindingly gorgeous woman on his arm like an accessory.

*Is Fields Done Playing the Field?*

"Oh my God," I mumble to myself.

Rolling my eyes, I take a tiny sip of the coffee to test its temperature, but I'm so distracted by my phone that my sip is more of a gulp.

*Too hot.*

The liquid burns the roof of my mouth, and I jolt, bumping right into another person.

I glance over with an apology on the tip of my tongue,

but the woman I ran into doesn't even spare me the opportunity.

Instead, she tosses a scathing glare my way, her plump red lips pouting like I spilled my coffee on her, even though I didn't.

Scoffing, I smooth my sweater down with my free hand and inspect for any damage, finding only a single brown spot over my chest. Relieved, I grab a napkin on the way out the door as the café continues filling up.

Stepping outside, I dab at the setting stain like it's enough to rid myself of it. The next thing I know, I hit a hard chest, causing my glasses to fall to the tip of my nose. The lid flies off my cup, and my morning caffeine boost spills down the front of me.

"Ah!" I jump back, holding my arms out. If I was in anything other than my thick turtleneck sweater, that shit would've left a brutal mark on my skin.

"I'm so sorry." Two large hands grip my elbows, steadying me. "Are you okay?"

Disoriented, I blink as he glances between me, over his shoulder, and then back at me, his teeth raking over his bottom lip. He shrugs in a sheepish manner similar to Graham when he's hiding something.

When I see the awful woman who bumped into me walking away behind him, her curvy hips in a skintight skirt, I can't help my scowl.

I've had enough of this morning.

It's my first day of being twenty-eight, and it sucks balls. I'm running on zero sleep, the coffee I spent more than an e-book's worth on just spilled down to my belly button, and my brother's annoying friend is crashing my family vacation.

On top of it all, this jerk was too busy checking out a woman instead of being more careful.

He holds his hands out. "Please. Let me buy you another coffee—"

"Don't bother." I wave him off and rush back inside, only to find the line is now three times as long as it was when I first arrived. *Great.*

"Hey, I'm really sorry." A gentle hand touches my arm, and when I turn, it's the guy from outside. He's wearing his hat low, and his eyes are still hidden behind Ray-Ban Aviators, even though we're inside now where the sun's not blinding us. "I should've been watching where I was going, but—"

"But a nice ass caught your attention, instead, right?" I blurt, adjusting my glasses and jutting my chin up.

His arm falls as we take a step up in line. "That's not what happened."

"Oh?" I cross my arms, unsure of why I'm even entertaining this conversation other than there's nothing else to do until I get my new cup of coffee. I'm not leaving here without it.

"A woman needed directions, so I gave her some. I was being a friendly New Yorker. You know, battling the stereotypes that we're prickly and rude."

I relax my stance a fraction, furrowing my brows.

"That's all. I just wanted to make sure she knew where she was going. She has a job interview and was nervous." He shrugs as if he did what any Good Samaritan would do.

And it's true. I don't know of many guys in the city other than Graham and my father who would help a stranger.

Maybe that's why the woman was rude. She was nervous and flustered because of a job interview. Of all people, I understand that very well. Many of my clients come to me in a big bundle of nerves right before their interview.

Which definitely makes me feel like I stepped in a pile of dog shit.

"Oh. I'm sorry..." My voice trails off as he starts to remove his sunglasses, but just when I'm about to glimpse the color of his eyes, he pushes them back into place again.

*Odd.*

I run my gaze over him, traveling from the top to the bottom of this stranger, trying to get a sense of him. His beard appears too scruffy for someone wearing a Harvard ball cap. His confident posture, on the other hand, is something I'd expect from a prestigious Ivy League grad— Graham's one of them, after all.

Even though half this guy's face is covered, there's something familiar about him. About his square jaw. His lean but sculpted frame. His touch on my elbow before should've felt foreign, but instead, it was something more than friendly.

I spot movement over his shoulder through the glass windows and notice a man outside with a large camera hung around his neck. He's peering inside the coffee shop like he's looking for someone.

Before I can think more of it, he walks away, shaking his head.

Can this morning get any weirder?

I blink the Harvard guy back into focus, gathering my thoughts. "Do I know you?"

He steps back, glancing around, then dips the hat lower over his forehead. "I don't think so."

"I feel like..." I shrug off any thoughts other than getting my hands on another cup of coffee and offer him a small smile. "Never mind."

He places his hand on my arm again, his touch confusingly warm and comforting. "Let me buy you another coffee. Maybe another sweater too?"

I shake my head. "Not necessary. I have extra clothes in my car."

"As all unsuspecting citizens should." He cracks a smile. Even though it's not enough to erase the worry from between his brows, it's a charming grin, nonetheless, one complete with perfectly straight white teeth and dimples.

*Fucking dimples.*

"I'll take you up on the coffee, though," I manage, tearing my attention away from the cute lines in his cheeks.

"After you." He spreads his arm to the side for me to continue forward in line.

My hand trembles as I gesture it over myself and say, "This is my fault too. To tell you the truth, I wasn't watching where I was going, either. And I shouldn't have assumed you were being a sleazy pervert checking out that woman."

He hangs his head, chuckling as he stuffs his hands into his jeans pockets.

"That's so not me." I wave my hands in front of my face like I'm denouncing the devil. "I don't know what came over me."

"Sounds like you know too many sleazy pervs," he teases, and I wish I could see his eyes. Would there be a twinkle in them? An amused look in them as we fall into this easy banter?

"They're everywhere, actually," I say, letting a soft laugh escape. "And right before I ran into you, I ran into a woman because I was on my phone. So stupid."

"It's a dangerous thing these days." He leans in to let a patron by, and the hint of his woodsy scent makes my mouth water more than the smell of coffee. We're now standing side by side, my shoulder to his bicep, and warmth radiates from him like heat from the fireplace at the cabin, drawing me in. "I swear, we act like we can't live without our phones, but people did just fine without them a hundred years ago."

I nod, my lips curling in the corners. "The sad part is, I wasn't even reading anything important."

His hat covers the top of his forehead, casting a shadow over his expression, but I imagine if I could see all of him, I'd see his brow lifted, his interest piqued. Why does he seem so familiar? My instinct that I know him fades even more as we talk, and that nagging itch is replaced by a tingling sensation. I'm overcome by it as though I've never seen a good-looking man before—half of one, anyway.

"Forget what I said. I love wasting time on my phone. Do tell what nonsense you were reading." He nudges me with his shoulder.

I laugh as we step forward, getting closer to the counter, my brown-stained shirt almost forgotten. I use my thumb to unlock my phone and turn the screen toward him. "I was reading dumb gossip."

"Oh?" His body tenses.

"I don't normally bother, but I had to check out the latest news on Manhattan's most beloved man-child." Rolling my eyes, I scroll down. "I mean, Carter Fields is almost forty years old and doesn't know the difference between the gas pedal and the brake. This guy has crashed his car way too often than is socially acceptable."

"There's a social standard for that sort of thing?"

I shrug. "I don't know, but three in a month is too many."

His perfect posture falters as he shifts on his feet. "I'm..." He clears his throat. "I mean, I heard Carter's only thirty-five."

"And I'm twenty-eight and a day," I tease, exaggerating my exact age.

"Besides, I hear this *man-child*, as you so eloquently put it"—he swipes the corners of his twitching lips—"does a lot of charity work. Very generous."

I make a noncommittal sound.

"Tell me, what types of men do you prefer, then?"

There's a trace of humor in his voice, but I almost don't notice it. Instead, I'm distracted by his full lips, the bottom one slightly bigger than the top. It gives him a unique charm.

I tuck my hair behind both ears as he stands firmly in place, his head tilted as he waits for my answer like it's important.

He's a very intriguing stranger, for sure, and I'm thrilled by the mystery of him. I'm even tempted to ask him to hang out here until I can unravel it.

I clear my throat, stepping forward in line. "Well—"

"What can I get you?" a high-pitched voice behind the counter interrupts.

I turn to my left, unnerved by the butterflies in my stomach. Surprisingly engrossed in this conversation, I didn't realize we were so close to the front.

Once we finish with our order—a new caffé latte for me and an Americano for him—he stands with me on the waiting side of the café and leans down. From this close, his cologne invades my senses, and it's easier for me to hear him when he says, "So? Tell me your idea of the perfect man. Your boyfriend, perhaps?"

I inhale a sharp breath like he asked what color my panties are. "No, no boyfriend. No perfect man, either, but if I meet him, I'll be sure to let you know."

"You'll give me your number, then? So you can let me know?" His hoarse voice is in my ear, sending shivers down my spine.

"I walked right into that one, didn't I?" I manage a small smile through the turmoil in my head and chest.

"Literally." He rocks backward on his heels, his wide grin victorious.

"Tessa?" the barista calls, setting a new latte on the counter.

"Tessa?" the mystery man repeats, and his previous smirk falls slack.

Guess he didn't hear me give my name to the barista when we ordered. It was loud, and the noise in here has only grown since we first stepped in line.

I want to ask him what his name is. I gave mine for both of our orders.

I want to give him my phone number too, but... I shouldn't.

"Um..." I grab our coffees, and once I hand him one, I lift mine to clink against his. "Thank you for the coffee, but I have to go."

"Right." He drops all humor and stills, facing me. It makes me feel like he's studying me, but I don't wait to find out. It wouldn't do me any good, anyway.

Waving over my shoulder, I weave through the line and dart out the door, my heart thundering. Once my feet hit the sidewalk and I suck in the fresh midmorning air, I run my hand through my short hair, bogged down like it's already late in the evening.

Who was I in there? So easily chatting with a good-looking guy while my stomach did backflips?

An immediate connection is what that was.

It's the one thing I've been actively trying to avoid for almost a year, but I can't deny how exhilarating it was.

*Shit.*

My phone vibrates in my hand, snapping me out of my trance.

*Graham.*

I take a sip of my coffee, pushing away thoughts of the Harvard guy's mouth so close to my ear. It's not normal to have such an extreme reaction to someone I don't know and will never see again. With a deep breath, I settle my nerves and ease the nagging knot in my stomach that can only be described as butterflies—unwanted as they are.

"You have some explaining to do, big brother." Holding the phone to my ear, I pick up the pace toward my car, but not before glancing behind me. I don't see the Harvard guy, though, and I'm more miffed than I should be.

The smart part of my brain says *good riddance.*

But the other part of me wonders why he didn't try harder for my number.

"Carter needs my help. I couldn't say no," Graham says, his voice soothing. He's used this tone on me all my life when he's needed a favor, whether it was to lie for him when he missed curfew or to be his designated driver on the rare occasion he goes out drinking. I've never been able to refuse him, and he knows it too.

I scoff. "And you thought a simple text to let me know he's going to be joining us would be enough for me not to lose it?"

"I was going to call after you had a chance to do your research and calm down."

"What do you mean?"

"I know you've already researched every exaggerated snippet of Carter's life in the media."

"I didn't realize I was so predictable." I turn the corner and walk between the lines of cars on the sides of the road until I reach mine.

"No, I just know you too well."

I carefully set my coffee in the cupholder and shut the car door behind me. "Well, I did do my research to see what your old friend has been up to since college, but I can't say it calmed me down."

Graham's voice drops when he says, "I know what people say about him, but he's not the immature asshole they make him out to be. Give him a chance."

I sigh. "He must be important enough for you to let him crash *my birthday*."

"I know, and I'll make it up to you. I didn't want you two to meet this way, either." He mumbles something, but he continues before I can ask for clarification. "I wouldn't do this if Carter didn't need me. We've had each other's backs since college, and he's saved my ass a few times. He never lets me forget one time in particular." He chuckles. "I swear, if I would've known what Trixie was up to—"

"Dr. Rollins, your ten o'clock is ready," another voice sounds from his end.

Graham addresses me again. "I need to go, sis."

"Wait, who's Trixie? And when is Carter supposed to—"

The line goes silent.

I chew my lip, holding in the rest of my sentence like a sneeze, and toss my phone to the passenger seat. That's the life of a physician—drop everything when it comes to a patient. I'm used to it from both Graham and our father. Before he retired, anyway.

His office is always bustling, and Graham and Dr. Blythe —his partner—run around it like the people on Wall Street, rushing from one patient to the next.

So, I let it slide each time Graham abruptly hangs up on me. What else can I do?

Checking my mirrors, I pull onto the road that will take

me out of New York and up past Hartford, Connecticut, the same road I used to take a few times a year. As always, I turn the volume on the pop station higher and let my mind drift as the tall buildings transform into trees.

My family and I go up to our cabin for holidays and birthdays, but I missed Labor Day. Graham's birthday was in June, but we didn't meet at the cabin since his schedule was too loaded. I've been too busy with work as well.

While I was in graduate school, though, I went up there to study or simply get away from real life, especially after my breakups with Wyatt.

He and I dated on and off for a year until I realized *off* was the better option for my sanity, and I filed that period of my life away under a "bad decisions" folder in my brain.

While we were together, Wyatt drove me crazy, but our chemistry was palpable. It was my first time getting sucked into an otherworldly feeling. One of passion and heat that made me constantly feel drunk in his presence.

That feeling was our downfall, though.

Merging onto the interstate, I laugh at myself. It's been a year since I last spoke to Wyatt, yet it feels longer. So much has happened since then. I'm another year older, with a real job and my own apartment in Brooklyn.

I've traded mind-blowing sex and an unhealthy relationship for the occasional *safe* man.

I pass signs for New Haven, and the closer I get to the cabin, the more my heart swells.

As shadows of trees dance across the hood of my car and windshield, happy nostalgia replaces the dread that usually comes with thinking of Wyatt. When I stop at the same gas station we always came to when I was a kid, I'm consumed by wistful memories. Dad would fill the car up, and Mom would get me juice and plain Lay's chips. She knew how much I hated the different flavors back then—a habit I grew out of as I got older.

I put my car in park next to one of the pumps, fill my tank up, and grab BBQ chips from inside. Once I'm on the road again, the city of Hartford in my rearview mirror, I admire the river, the trees covered in light reds and fading greens, and the air filled with early signs of fall.

I'm cautious as I drive down the winding road, careful of the steep drop-off where there should be a shoulder, until the cabin comes into view. I inch down the gravel driveway, and my breath hitches as I roll to a stop.

My family's quaint wooden cabin stands before me, two grand oak trees towering over it on either side like they're keeping it and my memories safe.

Leaving my bags, I get out and walk up to the porch where I run my fingers over the deep red window shutters. The white rocking chairs by the door are chipped and faded, but they're sturdy. In the past, Mom and Dad would sit out here in the mornings, sipping coffee and enjoying the sunrise while Graham and I would sleep. When we'd wake, we'd beg them to come inside for French toast, Mom's breakfast specialty.

Daniel and his wife, Marie, are the closest neighbors half a mile up the road. They're also good family friends. My parents probably called to let them know we'd be arriving today. They always grab these chairs from the shed out back and make sure the heat is turned on for us.

Once I'm seated in a chair, I open and close my eyes, enjoying the breeze on my cheeks like a soft caress.

Late September might be my favorite time of year. Even though the mornings and evenings are chilly, it's still warm during the day. Unlike midsummer, this is the perfect season since it's not so hot to melt ice cream.

Not everyone agrees, though. In the city, it seems early fall is colder for people who aren't native to the area, like some of my clients. I work with people from all around the world, and each fall, those from the South especially, come to me covered in enough thick winter gear to brave Mount Everest. It always makes me smile.

I'll miss my clients this week, but this will be a much-needed break to recuperate and bond with my family.

Smiling, I continue rocking, enjoying the peace this place offers, unlike the city. Birds flap their wings in the distance. The sun filters through the leaves on the trees. The air is fresh and hopeful as the new season settles upon us.

*Silence.*

Until a passing truck jolts me from my spot.

Exhaling with contentment, I return to the car for my bags, checking my phone on the way.

There's no word from Graham or my parents, but that's not unusual. They said they'll be here this evening, and they will be.

I hum as I grab my bags and mentally list the things I want to do before everyone else gets here. Who knows when the playboy will show.

As I make my way inside, I glance back at the mailbox at the end of the driveway. I have half a mind to tape off a protective perimeter around it before he arrives.

Snorting, I open the door, drop the bags at my feet, and take a deep breath. I inhale years of history and traditions, which I plan to keep intact as much as I can, starting with this week.

I close the door behind me and check the pictures along the walls and across the mantle above the fireplace as the memories continue to assault me.

Wyatt hated this cabin. One of his reasons was the

family pictures. He'd say he felt like my parents were watching us the entire time he and I would visit.

On top of that, he and Graham never got along. Their arguments were so childish, fighting over the last bag of chips or who would sleep on the couch since we only have three bedrooms. Wyatt knew he'd sneak into my room after Mom and Dad went to bed, but he just liked pushing Graham's buttons.

I had to play referee between them so often it made me dizzy.

Thank God I don't have to do that now. Beyond benefiting my own mental health, breaking up with Wyatt has helped Graham and me get to a much better place in our relationship.

All is as it should be now.

After an hour of welcomed silence, I'm halfway finished with my freshly brewed cup of decaf coffee and three chapters into the newest Nora Roberts romance when there's a knock on the door.

From my spot on the window seat, I peek through the blinds, but the man's back is to me. In the driveway, a Maserati is parked behind my Subaru, making me snicker. Only a spoiled billionaire would drive an expensive sports car through winding roads and down a gravel driveway without flinching.

I open the door, expecting the clean-cut pretty boy whose images are plastered all over the internet, but his black hoodie, the scruff along his jaw, and his unruly hair curling over his ears surprise me.

"I didn't know when you..." My voice trails off when I notice the Harvard ball cap and aviators.

"Hey, Tessa." He flashes his dimples, but instead of

causing a jolt of welcomed electricity like they did this morning, they send me into a panic.

All air leaves my lungs, and my knees buckle.

"Oh my God." I slam the door in his face and lock it. How the hell did the coffee shop guy find me all the way up here?

Did he… follow me?

"Oh my God," I mutter again, my heart racing.

"Tessa?" His voice is muffled by the barrier between us and also the blood rushing to my ears.

With trembling hands, I grab my phone from the couch and dial Sheriff Thompson. "It's Tessa. I need your help at the cabin." There's more knocking on the door, and suddenly, I can't breathe. "Please hurry."

*Keep reading Stuck with the Billionaire on Amazon and free in Kindle Unlimited!*

## ACKNOWLEDGMENTS

Thank you for reading! If you met Graham in Stuck with the Billionaire and were curious for his HEA, I hope it was everything you expected, and more! If you're meeting Graham for the first time in this little novella, I hope you enjoyed his and Isabel's love story too.

I'm so excited to have participated in this 12 Days of Kissmas series with such an amazing group of authors! It has been a blast.

Big thanks to my editor Amanda for helping this story shine. You've made me a stronger writer, and I so appreciate you.

To my KKSB girls—this 12 Days of Kissmas came about so randomly and gloriously last year. I'm so happy to think up crazy fun things to do together for amazing readers. Cheers to many more collabs and fun times in The Steam Room.

Another big thanks goes to my mom for loving holiday romances as much as I do. Every year, I look forward to watching all the sweet Hallmark Christmas movies with you, and it's part of the reason I enjoy writing these kinds of romances (with added steamy flair ;))

To my husband—as I always say, our story is my favorite love story, and I appreciate your support and encouragement to keep chasing this writing dream. Love you, forever and always.

# ABOUT THE AUTHOR

Georgia Coffman is an author of steamy contemporary romance. She has a Master's in Professional Writing and loves the TV show *Friends*, as well as shopping. She and her husband enjoy working out and playing with their two pups. Georgia loves to connect on social media or through email, so feel free to reach out with any questions, your fave book recommendations, or even a funny joke!

Newsletter
Facebook
Instagram
TikTok
Pinterest

Goodreads
BookBub
Amazon
Verve Romance
The Steam Room

Manufactured by Amazon.ca
Bolton, ON

22398604R00069